Lenny

'Hey, Lenny.' Big Cop. Hand on Lenny's arm.

'Comere Lenny, the Sergeant says he wants I should bring you down to the station house.'

'Again?' It was getting to be a number. Do a show, get arrested, get bailed out, do another show . . .

'What's it this time?' he wants to know. Ever since the last bust he's so clean, he could sing TV soap commercials.

'What makes you think you got a right to use a word like that in a public place?'

'What word, officer? I said a lot of words.'

Lenny

Valerie Kohler-Smith

Based on the film written by
Julian Barry

 TANDEM

Originally published in the United States by Grove Press, Inc., 1974

First published in Great Britain by Tandem Publishing Ltd, 1975

Tandem Books are published by Tandem Publishing Ltd, 14 Gloucester Road, London SW7. A Howard & Wyndham Company.

Made and printed in Great Britain by
Hunt Barnard Printing Ltd, Aylesbury, Bucks.

CHAPTER 1

THE WOMAN SITS ON A DAY BED, LOOKING LIKE HER better days had long since gotten away from her. Her hair kind of hangs there, with no particular color about it. It must have been brighter. A real red probably. It's hard to tell now—through the henna, the persistent graying, the stupor of city filth that has gotten such a grip on it.

Still her face is bony. She's got great wide peasant cheekbones. And a kind of through-it-all innocence that still lives in the eyes. Honey Bruce, who used to be married to Lenny. Who a lot of people say ruined his life. Who, a lot of other people say, never had that much grip on it. Honey Bruce, whose big number these days is being interviewed by any Lenny-o-phile who can up a little bread for her to look back a little and remember what she can. Whatever she can face.

"Oh, I would say—ah, let's see—"

She's got a low voice and as she talks she fishes through a box of pictures and letters. She talks to her feet. She looks off into the room.

"Yeah, he was busted at least nine or ten times. Twice for possession of narcotics. And, ahhh—three, maybe four times for—for obscenity."

She fishes for something in the box, and doesn't find it. She looks down at the tape recorder which just keeps going. Round and round, round and round. Just like things—

CHAPTER 2

THINGS WITH LENNY—

You know Lenny Bruce. Tits and Ass? Guys are Carnal? The Palladium?

Come on, you saw him at some cellar somewhere. Or if you're too young, you've got a record.

Dirty Lenny, with the funny mouth and the tracks up his arm.

The people at table four are breaking up. The woman behind them has just put on her glasses so she can hear better. The MC has spoken the words: Ladies and gentlemen—Lenny Bruce. And Lenny, with the beard, with the dark shadows under his eyes,. has leaned his cheek against the mike, given the audience their moment to give him the hard look and then opened up on them.

"You know that Eleanor Roosevelt gave Lou Gehrig the clap?" And who's not gonna laugh?

It's the sixties. Lenny don't fool around with the Vaughan Monroe *shtick* anymore. When he comes on now, it's to show up the guy who thinks through his

7

hard hat, the dame who don't know an orgasm from a French poodle. Ever since Lenny found out who he was and where it was hiding, he's been letting everybody have it. Right between the laughs.

Come on, the point is—the suppression of words. Look—here it is 1964, and every doctor I know tells me that "a certain disease" is on its way to becoming an epidemic again when one good shot in the ass would knock it out. But still it's on the rise. Why? 'Cause nobody talks about it. Nobody even wants to say the word. In fact, when the Community Chest hits on you, do you say, "Excuse me, but how much of my buck is going for the clap?"

"The guy's a gas," somebody says to somebody else. At another table they're poking each other with elbows. Yeah, they're smiling, yukking and shaking their heads. But they're not saying "clap" either. They do dues with Lenny. Let him say it for them.

So O.K., a boy gets the clap. Can he go to his father?

Why don't you ask him? He's sitting over there behind the *Chivas Regal.* "Who, me?" he snorts. "Lettim try it." His kid; he pulls some dumb ass stunt like clap. What the fuck did he pay all these years to send him to Dalton?

Or even the hip couple with the shades and hookah. They *get* clap. They don't go around broadcasting it. Yeah—Lenny knows and he runs with it.

Relate to his father? The kid's lucky if he can go to some jerk who sweeps up a drugstore:

BOY WITH CLAP: Hey, Manny, mop later. Can I talk to you?
MANNY: Whuh?
KID: I got the clap.
MANNY: You? Gowan—where'd you get it?
KID: Painting a car, *shmuck*—what's the difference?
MANNY: So whuddya want from me?

KID: Gimme some pills. You work around the stuff all day long.

MANNY: Well, awright—here.

KID: (reading label) Dexedrine spansules. Is this good?

MANNY: Yeah, it's all the same horseshit. Keeps you awake so you know you got it.

KID: O.K. Reason I want these is I gotta good job, you know, so I don't wanna get laid off.

MANNY: Oh yeah. Where ya workin'?

KID: The meat-packing plant. You want a couple of steaks?

MANNY: No!! Just burn the doorknobs on the way out.

Right? Sure, right. So right away Lenny's into his own voice again, and he's broken-field *shticking*.

See—we have to start talking about it. And what we have to do is get some of our past national heroes that have had it to admit it. Okay, Eleanor Roosevelt gave Lou Gehrig the clap!!! Yeah, gave it to Chiang Kai-shek too—and then he gave it to J. Edgar Hoover, which is how it really spread.

Are you kidding?

Listen maybe one day Jerry Lewis would go on television and he'd have a clap-a-thon. Or you know those little old ladies with the bridge tables and chairs? shakin' those tin cans? "Help the clap. Please sir—help the clap." Yeah, wild. Only it'll never happen. Because talking about it, saying the word, makes you the worst *shmuck* in the community, right?

Again, right. Then how come Lenny's got such a following? How come he can live in that big fancy house on the Hollywood hill? How can he afford so many hangeroners. So many ten, twenty and a hundred percenters?

9

CHAPTER 3

HONEY CLOSES HER EYES AS THE INTERVIEWER ASKS HER about Baltimore. About how she met Lenny. About the beginning of things.

"Lemme think. It was maybe '50 or '51. I was starring. I was—"

She laughs, the word starring. Comeon, she says, to herself, let's hear it for the way it was.

"Well, I was working in this club. You know—"

And if the interviewer didn't know, he didn't have to. At least he'd been to a lot of movies.

Harriet Lloyd, born Jollis, the piece with the knockers playing the same upholstered armpit she'd worked in from there to Detroit. Lookit her legs, legs that kept right on going and then more of them; blinding white, up so far they were imbedded in her adenoids. Otherwise known as Hot Honey, up under the lights. While the duPont slavies could feel her snatch right

10

through their eyeballs—her round white belly, pink-nippled suckers, down there pumping on their own yangoes, under their jackets, under their evening *Baltimore Dailies*. Honey bumping, grinding, hipping and thrusting, showing thigh, running hands over all that white flesh smothered in hot light. That red-headed, softer than goosedown flesh. Flesh they needed—flesh they came crosstown, uptown, anytime to pretend with. Flesh they had to have, paid through the nose for while smaller-time flesh got them to have another drink, got them to buy and buy some more, got them hungrier and hungrier with no end in sight.

Flamingo.

The gravel-gutted sax roared on and then more *Flamingo*.

Dirty music. Dirty lady. Dirty, I love it, when she showed ass, when she leaned over just so far, too far, not far enough. And then the sequined harlot up the ramp again, her tongue wet around her mouth, her eyes soaked from sweat and juices and you-know-what, back there, mister, just for you and me, and me, and me, and then another glove. A glove dangled over the big Polack with the nose pores, over the steamfitter with the ruptured hernia, and then over to the shill who seen it so many times: "get it over with, baby, let's move."

She spread her arms, one still yellow from a finger-less over-the-elbow, and again she leaned over and again those knockers they shimmied a little left, a little right, imagine those knockers around your cock, around your ears, stopping all sight, all sound, as they smothered you—as everybody went wild. As that slippery yellow glove slid down that pillow arm, as that mocking face stared straight through their eyeballs. As again the belly slithered forward, sucked itself back. As the smoke rose and the yells built. As they let loose, these suckers, these rack-em-up, jack-em-up big time spenders, had another and another, rolled out the

11

bills, got harder than their old ladies ever saw or wanted. As Honey, when she knew she had 'em, moved in closer and swung that ass meaner.

Who gives a shit.

"Three more hours," Hot Honey thought to herself, running her tongue across her teeth. She was getting down to the bra. With the shimmies, with the sequins, with the fringes that were wearing thin, she'd have to get down to the Woolworth's tomorrow and fix herself up another layer. Three more hours and she'd be off.

And the jerks were getting restless. She pulled herself up, threw out her tits and shook them nonstop for two minutes, as they whistled, as they stomped, as they reached out to grab an ankle or maybe just a touch of her three-inch heel.

She looked down on these guys, what she could see of them, through the smoking haze of the gels in her face. They were out there, she could feel them. "Lay 'em out, sweetheart," they yelled at her. "Mmmm, an' ain't they the sweet ones." Hell, she knew they were out there; a bunch of losers, a bunch of real nice family men. They were out there and they loved her and two more strips and she'd be down to her panties and G. She'd make it good. She'd make it slow. She'd make them slobber for it. She'd run her hands over her nice round tits. She'd lie down and swivel her bones. She'd rub some more. And some more after that.

She wasn't called Hot Honey for nothing.

Lenny's about to meet Honey. He's gonna see her in a cafeteria. She's gonna see him. It's gonna be like a million boy meets girl movies. Lenny's gonna know right away, OHBOY, is that terrific? Is that some piece? Would I like to crawl between that? If only I weren't such a green, wet-eared, jewboy fuckup-with-the-broads. Jewboy fuckup scared shy on accounta Sally, on accounta Mama. On accounta all the lousy bringing up I got brought up on.

Lenny with the bright-eyed look in his young face.

Lenny before the dirt in his mouth. Before he knew where much of anything was at, but then what could you expect—

Before there was Lenny Bruce, there was a sort of fat kid whose sheik eyes and sleek beauty were lost inside matzoball cheeks. The kid's name was Lenny Schneider and his mother had ants in her pants; special showbiz ants. His mother lived to be "on." To have lights in her eyes, fishnet on her legs (she had good legs), and the old smell of greasepaint up her pre-fixed nose.

Which meant, because she was divorced early on from Lenny's father, Myron Schneider, Lenny got, you know, dumped a lot while Mama: Sally, Sally Marr, sometimes Sally Marsalle, sometimes Boots Malloy, originally Sadie Kitchenberg, while she went off to her gigs. To her life.

So what was Lenny's life?

Halls with the smell of wet mops. Iceboxes with pans underneath to catch the drips. Nicked enamel sinks. Toilets with spongy black mold around the stems. The sounds of other people sleeping in the next room, in the same room. Chenille bathrobes with the roses worn salmon-colored. Douche bags with stiffened hoses. And never the same halls and never the same bathrobes. Cousin's. Friend's.

"Look, she's a young woman yet. You can't expect she should give up her whole life." With the Kitchenbergs, one hand washed the other one. And what were they going to do? Let the kid run loose in the streets? So Lenny got used to a lot of Tanta Richels down the hall. A neighbor's Uncle Laiseh. A Pinya. A Velvil. Sometimes waking up in an unfamiliar kitchen next to an ironing board with scorched sheets pinned to it. Playing immys with a kid named Shrully one day, Hummy, Yabo the next.

But mostly he went to Sadie's sister, Mema.

13

"Look, by the *goyim* she can parade around, all of a sudden Sally. But by Mema, a sister is a Sadie."

With Mema there was no hoity-toity. Mema was always the one who was there. To smother the boy with her beet-juicy breasts. To have a chance of her own to be a mother.

A good soul, Mema, you could always count on her, but a *kvetch un a krenk*—If she didn't get off his back he'd *plotz* from her, Mema.

Mema mixed her love with more *bubbameises* than Lenny ever learned to cope with. Thirty-something years later he was still giving off the flavor of her paranoia in his "flasher" routine. The woman who feeds the chicken soup is a hard woman to wrench from your heart. Even if she was a pain in the ass. And not only Lenny's.

"I wouldn't cut off my hands for you Sadie? But you'll tell me—what's so terrible? So you'll take a week. Two weeks. You'll sit home, we'll *shmoose*. Sadie, the boy should know he has a mother. Be a person already—it's enough with the show business."

Except it wasn't ever enough. The showbiz in Sally Marr's blood was a disease. And Lenny caught it.

Still, it wasn't all Sally's fault Lenny didn't have what the Hygiene-class textbook called "a good home."

"What's the matter with the father?" they used to say around the neighborhoods. "Mr. High-and-Mighty Schneider, the college boy? That's by you the way for a grown man with a son he should *tummel* in the streets day and night?"

And even after Micky Schneider did take him, when Lenny was eleven. After Micky Schneider scrimped, saved, remarried and got custody.

"It's a sin and a shame," they still said, because "by eleven it's too late already. Some day that boy'll do something terrible."

Too many of other people's wet dreams had stained the membranes of his eyes. His childhood had already been marked. By eleven years old you have any idea how many nights Lenny Schneider had forced himself up past *Henry Aldrich, Inner Sanctum* and *America the Beautiful* so he could listen in on the heavy breathing all around him. His world was filled with too many strangers crowded into too few rooms.

The sounds of third cousins brushing their partials.

The smells of somebody's uncle-by-marriage's socks.

A kid gets scars from that kind of knowing that no paper route in the world can set to rights.

No matter how assiduously Micky Schneider sets out to spoil him rotten.

He was already spoiled for clipped lawns and regular hours.

He was already as rotten as French cheese. What is he some kind of fool? It's too late for balloon-tired bikes, for Jack Armstrong the All American *Putz*.

By the time Lenny was eleven he'd spent too much time on the other side of somebody's studio couch waiting for whoever it was that night to turn to whoever else it was:

"Comeon."

For her to turn to him:

"I don't wanna."

"What do you mean, you don't wanna?"

"I don't wanna, that's what I mean, I don't wanna."

"Two nights in a row? We didn't yesterday either."

"So sue me. We didn't yesterday either."

"So how come?"

"So how nothing."

And then maybe the rustle of him moving towards her. The rustle of her poking him in the ribs with her elbow.

"He'll hear us," she whispers.

"So he'll hear us. What am I supposed to do stop living? Let him hear us." The rustle of him shlurping her breast. The clearer sound of her laughing.

"Maybe he'll learn something," he says; except there was no maybe about it. When it came to learning, the kid was a vacuum cleaner. A genuine Hoover.

And no father's Long Island in the world was going to homogenize that.

The years piled up. Lenny dropped out of school, left the house on Long Island and went in search of his world. The war came along. He thought maybe he'd join the Navy and see a couple of geisha girls, which brought Myron in search of Sadie (though it killed him). After all he'd done for the boy, taken him off the streets when she wouldn't lift a finger, done for him, broken his ass—and who had won out in the end? Sally and her *fablunged* nightclubs.

"What do you mean you don't want Lenny to join the Navy?" Her tone was the worst. What did she mean, what did he mean? Who else had a right? Did *she,* one day, sit home with the chicken pox? The measles in the black room? The mumps so bad his eyes were swollen shut?

In all those years had she changed one iota? (Never mind the sequins, the snood or the pointed nails that shone in the dark.)

"The truth doesn't mean any more to you today than it ever did."

"Again with the truth. You know a person could *plotz* with you, Micky. Always with the concepts. Truth. Fairness. No wonder Lenny ran away from you. You don't know *zilch* how to move through this world, Micky Schneider, and you never will."

"Sally, he's a baby."

"Some baby. Listen, philosopher, that baby has more sense in his *tush* than—*oy,* what's the use to talk, Micky. Sit down a minute. Have a cup of coffee. Eye to eye, you and I will never—"

"The use of talking, may I remind you, is the only way we humans have devised for communicating." And so it went, apples and oranges soaking in oil and water, Myron and Sadie, Micky and Sally, the same as when they were married. Two eyewitnesses at a house on fire. One saw with his own eyes the pyromaniac. The other heard the sounds of the oily rags ignite.

"Why should he *pish* his life away?" The father in uniform. Wasn't one life per family per war enough for one's country?

"The trouble with you, Micky." Mama, The Personality Kid. "Everything is a big tragedy. I'm telling you Lenny has moxie. He'll live. Have a piece of *shnecken*. Your favorite—with the pecans. He'll live, he'll have himself a little ass, he'll think things over. Don't be such a worrier, *sit*. She wouldn't catch you, your wife. What's her name?"

"Her name is Dorothy. You know her name is Dorothy and she's not looking to 'catch' me. She's a wonderful person."

"Did I say she wasn't? Have another pecan—and never mind about your wife, what do I care what she is, your typist—"

"Now see here, Sally, I didn't come here to—"

"Oh, drink your coffee, Myron. We won't discuss your precious Dorothy. Your princess."

"So where is he?"

"You're asking me?"

"And who else should I ask? When does he come to see his father? Does he send me a postcard? Where is he, Sally?"

"What am I, his keeper? Where is he? He comes. He goes. But I'll tell you one thing—you ought to see him, Micky. He's on his way. One day they'll all hear from him."

"Who? Who'll hear? Sally, what is it with you? First how should you know where he is—and then, I ought to see him. I ought to see him where?"

"The club, lunkhead—the club."

A low groan from Lenny's father. A groan that had been festering in his gut ever since he first realized his ex-wife had been bitten by a dressing room.

And now his son. Don't tell him any more. Next to show business, the Navy was almost medical school.

"So he craps out—"

"Who, as you say, 'craps out,' Sally? Who?" Micky cuts another piece of *shnecken* and dunks it into his coffee absentmindedly. It's the cobra fascinated by the soprano recorder. He doesn't want to listen. He has to.

"The MC, Micky, the MC—aren't you listening? One day the sonavabitch just doesn't show and Lenny went on instead. Micky, the kid was sensational. He killed them, I tell you one day he'll have his name in lights. I can see it now: 'The one and only Lenny Bruce.'"

"Bruce? Who's Lenny Bruce?"

"Oh comeon Micky, you don't think for one minute you'll read up in lights, 'The one and only Lenny Schneider?'"

So at the cafeteria, when Lenny first laid eyes on Honey's hair down to her *pupick* and some chick said, "Gowan, it's fake"—from what did he have to base a comparison? What did Lenny know from a real anything? All he knew was he saw the most wonderful creation of his life sitting across from him giving him the eye. And that's all he wanted to know.

CHAPTER 4

FROM THE NAVY TO *The Club Charles*. FROM LEN-neleh Schneider to Lenny Bruce. The little kid with the chubby cheeks has smoothed out. He's dap. He's ruffled up the front, has himself a lean and hungry look and has started in the biz with a rented tux, and eleven big name impressions.

It's somehow gotten to be 1951 and Lenny's in Baltimore. *The Club Charles* is straight out of every B movie on the lot. There's the broad in the sequins and marcelled head at the eighty-eight ivories, crooning her number straight for the club owner who's banging her. There's the watered booze and the B girls who don't even drink that, spilling their tea into the rug to keep the suckers buying. Lenny's on next, armed with the Joe Miller joke book approach to a world he only knows from his mama's fishnet knees. But it's the blueprint for success—right? Where all the "names" got their start, on the road between West Lind and anywhere.

"Look, I had problems as a kid," he starts. "It wasn't

till I was eight years old, I figured out my name wasn't 'Shut up!' "

Funny?

Forget it. Even a pro couldn't move this collection of types.

The guys married to somebody else who were too busy being not recognized.

Their dames, dangling their necklines for maybe a couple packs of cigarettes and enough left over for bobby socks for the kid.

A siding salesman from Toledo and the polka-dotted drunk who falls off the stool promptly at quarter of eleven.

Nevermind, Lenny moves into Barry Fitzgerald from *Long Voyage Home*. He puts on the glasses and gets the tiny pipsqueak brogue.

But whadya know—there she is, the looker from the cafeteria, the redhead with the solid gold ass. And she thinks he's smooth. Ass? He never saw ass like that in his life ever, welded to pants so tight and so shiny he had to stare into the spotlight to keep from going blind.

"O.K., folks, how about I do a little Bob White for you?" And he's into a bird call, taking in the girl's hair. Oh, it was real all right. The longest. The reddest. Slick, clean, *shtupping*—hair, baby, and he's *plotzing* up there as he slides into Jimmy Stewart which comes out with too much Cary Grant smothered in Marlene Dietrich, and then fast, to recoup with a smidge of Ronald Coleman and H.B. Warner from *Lost Horizon*.

"This is what you dragged me over here for?" the good-looking stud with the good-looking girl asks her. "A couple of bird calls and a guy with a beak on him to match?"

"Go on, invite him. I think he's cute."

"Some cute." As Lenny shifts into a Durante fedora and the Shnozola's fake nose, which doesn't quite make it either.

"Comeon," the guy says to the girl, but she's not going anywhere. She's got her eyes welded to Lenny.

"Hey," he says to the deafening silence out there, "is this any way to treat a veteran? Where were you *shmucks* when I was at Anzio and Salerno I'd like to know?" He'd like to see *them* up here rolling in the yuks. He hates them, the *momsahs,* and rolls up his sleeve so they can see a tattoo of an American flag.

Honey pokes the guy she's with.

"So, go on," she says. "It's almost over."

And it is. Lenny's into Vaughan Monroe. He's racing with the moon, and Honey Harlow's going to be sure he's there after, at the party at Eddie's. Where she'll be. Everything should work out by accident. You know? Like she knows from nothing.

"Comeon," she says again. "Be a good Joe. You won't be sorry," and she leans forward so Eddie can get a better look at what's in it for him.

"O.K., O.K., already," he says. But he knows he will be sorry, and the next thing Lenny knows it's bodies and more bodies, everybody draped around everybody else like fur collars. A party. With guess-who with her long gold legs crossed, in her sweetheart neckline showing her boobs up-and-at-'em, with that rosy scrubbed look on her.

Everybody's high. Everybody's happy. The Yard Bird's comin' in with *Groovin' High.* There's weed, ice cream and plenty of Yoohoos. There's even some smack and Lenny can finally relax. Nothing better than a boss bust to take the taste of the hard grind out of his mouth.

He's a little floaty. Easy, but keeping his orbs on that gorgeous fluff. She's been signaling him all night. The extra heavy tilt of the boobs in his direction, the green flashes, on and on again like a four-way Go. And him? He's foaming at the fly, blind from the cock up. This is one jive redhead.

And then the big signal. Her drink is empty. His moment. He's next to her in a flash. Smells *J&B,* takes

21

the glass and while filling it up, puts on *Shaw Nuff* cause that's what's gonna be with this doll. He can feel it down where it counts.

"Hey," he whispers to Artie. Artie goes where Lenny goes. Artie, who's always there when Lenny needs, wants, has to have something, you name it, in a hurry.

"Is that a winner face? A cross between a kindergarten teacher and a $500-a-night hooker?"

But before Artie can tell him, "Don't cross with her, Lenny, she's a cross to the bread basket," he's off. He's got the drink, he's got a Camel. He's even got a reefer. Whatever she wants is Jake with Lenny. With that *goyisha punim* on her, all she has to do is point.

"Hot Honey Harlow? That's really your name?" (A make-believe *shiksa* birthday present.)

He wants to know if maybe she wants to go out for a breath of fresh air. He wants to know if he can walk her home.

They go out and walk first in one direction and then in another.

Lenny takes Honey's hand.

"How does your old lady feel about your headlining in a strip joint?"

"What do you mean, how does she feel? I'm good."

"Gotta be a stronger word for what you are, baby," he thinks, then stops walking like he's going to kiss her. Then he panics—they walk on.

"Hey," he says, "what's your real name?" as he feels her pointy nails in the palm of his hand. He looks up and down the row of houses and wants everybody to get out of bed to see him in his tux holding the lady in the see-through skin.

"Well, all I can tell you is it wasn't till I was eight years old I found out my name wasn't—"

"Hey—watch that stuff, I sue easy. Besides it's eighty-six on that show tonight. I'd rather talk about you."

Forever. He already had the sense of her coating his teeth like a chocolate malted. He wanted to kiss her again, and got so jazzed up from the thought of the taste of her he did what he always did when he got high. He started to talk.

"You know, I don't even know how I got into this business. You think I like Baltimore? Hell, I should have been a pediatrician."

"A what?"

"Feet, baby—a bunion specialist. Let's see yours—I'm starving."

And the next thing he knows he's imagining licking her toes that stick out from her leopard mules like ten little tits, and makes an eating sound.

"You know you're crazy?" she giggled, pressing a look up against his eyes.

"Why not? My mother was a comic. Yeah, I guess that's why I am—showbiz was closer at hand than feet."

"Who's your mother?"

"You never heard of her. Anyway, when I got out of the Navy I changed my name—which reminds me you never told me yours."

"How do you know I never heard of her? I didn't know you were in the Navy."

"Yeah? Well, I was, and Sally Marr's my mother. Marr's not her real name, it used to be Schneider. Mine too. Actually Sally's not her real name either."

"Why'd she change it?"

"Are you kidding me? Sadie Schneider in lights? Or for that matter Lenny? Too Jewish, man. Too Jewish."

"Oh, is Schneider a Jewish name?"

"Is—Oh, Honeygirl, is my Aunt Mema gonna *shvitz* from you." And this time he did kiss her. Up against the double doors of her hotel. She kissed him back. And there we are back on another B movie set.

They go in and there's Elija Cook, Jr., at the desk, ready to snitch on anybody at the drop of a threat. There's the four-and-a-half-watt bulb in the lobby. The two-and-a-half in the stairwell and the wilted

23

palm fronds and Grand Rapids orientals.

"Anyway, I like the name Bruce. It reminds me of a captain of a football team, you know?"

Honey walks a little in front of him. He watches her porch swing as if his retinas are connected to its supporting chains.

"The president of the student council, even?"

"You hit it," he said, catching up to her. "Two weeks after I changed it, my mother was invited to join the DAR."

"418, please," Honey says to Elija, and then turns to Lenny. "What hotel are you staying at?"

His turn to stick out his hand.

"621." He shrugs.

The hot hand of Fate? A sign from the great beyond? Or just the joint all the small-time showbiz *shlubs* stayed at. Anyway it was worth a laugh and a sit in the lobby on a broken wicker divan, or davenport, or whatever it was they called a couch in Baltimore.

"So, anyway, about you? Don't tell me. it says, Hot Honey Harlow on your birth certificate—along with your little footprints, your little handprints and your little G-string prints—"

"You know I've changed it so many times even I can hardly remember anymore."

"Too Jewish, huh?"

And a big smile. A shake of that gorgeous *goyisha punim* of hers and a, "Oh Lenny, you're crazy" (the second of many).

"No, tell me."

"Harriet."

"Harriet?"

"You hate it?"

"No, no—it's a groove, Harriet—Leonard and Harriet—"

"Yeah. Just like those little matchbook covers people leave laying around on their coffee tables. With the gold letters."

He can't control himself. He reaches out and touches Harriet's long silken hair. Red like—like what? All he could think of was "tonsils." Red like tonsils? He started to laugh. Honey doesn't notice. She's fishing in her bag to find the key to her room.

And as he takes the key and reaches out for her as well he thinks of: harvest moon, bonfire, apples and oranges, bloodshot eyes and collies. But best of all, and what's wrong with it, he thought of tonsils. Why? he wondered. Why did the red of her hair hit him so hard it brought back childhood and all its traumas? His future and all its who-knows?

CHAPTER 5

HE CAN'T BELIEVE IT. *Stairway to Paradise* STARRING
Lenny Schneider as David Niven—and all in red-
headed technicolor. Loving her so easily. From "hello"
to "mind if I stop in for a minute," like that? Like
perfect? Like just the way he'd dreamed it would be
with a girl like her for how long?

"I just can't believe it," he kept saying. "Me and
you, you and me. Doing it, having it. Have I told
you lately, you're my birthday present? You're what I
want for St. Swithen's Day? The Ides of March?"

And he kept running in and out of the room. To
pee. To brush his teeth. The third time coming back
with his face foaming with lather. Which is when he
fell on her again.

"Harriet and Leonard on our bathroom hand
towels—for 'company,'" he said, kissing her, foam all
over her bellybutton, biting her belly to boobs.

He was wild about her. Wild and high. Lenny
Bruce didn't need to take anything—no bennies, no
dex, no nothing. Not a whiff. Not a snort. The only

thing Lenny would get high on was organic Honey, right from her very own pot.

Paradise all right, even in that *drecky* dump of a hotel room, with the wallpaper all over his eyes. (A rap in the kisser, that wallpaper. The iron bed. The same fourth-hand vanity he'd lived with in how many cousins' bedrooms? Except that this time it had turned into the room of his dreams.

"It's nuts," he murmured. "You, in the sack with me. I don't get so lucky. I'm Crazy Sally's kid, the one under the park bench with his thumb up his nose. I don't end up with the girl."

"Oh yeah," she whispered, running her fingers through his lathered chin, "Tell it to the Marines."

"No, I'm giving it to you straight. Between my mother and my *meshugeneh* Aunt Mema—I'm telling you, they had this blueprint. How to screw up a sex life in six easy steps. Especially, I had the nerve to come out with a pecker between my legs. I was one of the enemy, right?"

"I don't know, Lenny. You tell me."

Was she kidding? He'd tell everybody. Eventually. In one routine. In five routines. Sex. Aunts. Mothers. Lenny was working it all out. The funny ooze under the sore scabs.

"They were always warning me, you know, what would happen if I looked at a girl. What would happen if I touched? With the fingers? Are you kidding? Remember what happened to Schrully *Oy Gevult*— You know I was eight years old before—"

"I know, I know—before you realized *Oy Gevult* wasn't his last name."

"Hey, how does a *shiksa* like you know from *Oy Gevult*?"

"You think you're the only Jewboy got the hots for red hair?"

"Oh??? A yid freak, huh? My own little from-now-on private yid freak." And he kissed her again, his mouth full of it.

The long silky red cornsilk every kid from the other side of the Mediterranean yearns after. He kissed it and through it, her. He stared, pawed and adored. All that white and rosy young veal flesh on her. So lean and round. So tender—all covered with that fine salmon down. He adored her no different than a Guatemalan Mamacita before the holy blue madonna draped with lace valentines and St. Sebastian medals.

"Hit me," he screamed. "Hit me again," this instant Honey-junkie.

"I wanna go right now—I wanna go—I wanna go—" Screaming and pulsing, the two of them until they both shrieked, they both clung to one another and they both came as if shot through the ventricles with amyl nitrite. The Valhalla Express.

And then the heavy weight of a dead man on her. The fall and finish of a man spent of everything but the odor. Honey breathed him in. She wrapped her body around his legs, and they lay there like that for maybe four lifetimes, till Lenny broke the stillness with the sound of a lump in his throat.

"Well, man," he said, "I'm sorry—maybe next time I'll come through for you."

"What?" she said, looking up into those squid black holes in his eyes. "What?" through a well of total contentment.

"I hate to let a woman down, and all, but I guess they really got to me, you know—my aunt and my mother. I guess a guy can't hear how it'll fall off if he sticks it in without some of it rubbing off on him. So hey, man—can you ever forgive me?"

Forgive? What forgive? This spent wet seal with his "poor me" routine.

"You're real crazy—aintcha, Lenny Bruce?" she said, grabbing his black curly hair and shaking him.

Some forgive? She hadn't come off like that since never.

"Yeah," he growled, grabbing for her throat like a

vampire coming off a three-night fast. "But you dig it, right?"

"What do you think?" her long white legs wrapped around his guts. Her big soft breasts pressed so hard into his chest, he could feel them bulge right through his backbone.

CHAPTER 6

SEEING THROUGH TO THE SHIT. THAT'S WHY LENNY made it with the blinders-off set. That's why it hurt him, all the crap you have to wade through every day.

How do you really feel about *doing it?* You people out there—isn't that about the dirtiest thing we can do to each other? It's really *shmutzy, doing it.* Right? I mean what's the worst thing you can say to anybody? "Fuck you, Mister," huh? I mean it's weird. Comeon—if I really wanted to hurt you I should say "Unfuck you, Mister," shouldn't I? Isn't "Fuck you" really the best? O.K., figure this:

(He pantomimes being on the telephone.)

Hello ma? It's me. Hey listen—fuck you, ma. Sure I mean it. Hey, where's Pop? Put him on. Hey Pop? Hey, fuck you, Pop.

(Here he gets real slurpy sentimental.)

Hey listen you guys: if I don't make it home for Christmas and you see the Scheckners, tell 'em I said to gô fuck themselves. Cause I really dig them a lot. O.K.?

Sure. O.K. By the time Lenny was really into his own they figured they finally had a mouthpiece.

Finished for good were the old Schnozola routines, Vaughan Mon-Schneider and the rest of the set pieces he'd grown up with. Lenny had finally turned his life "on" stage, reversing Sally's inability to turn the stage off her's. Everything that ever happened to him had long since been stored, sifted and reshaped into a *shtick*. Being a Jew, sending off for a Captain Midnight decoder, the colored guy who hadn't yet turned black. The bit about Aunt Mema and Mama, the two nutzy Jewbroads who brought him partway up on a diet of scaring the shit out of him about sex. Finally Lenny stood back from it all and saw how it could all be used. How it could all be translated into Every-*shmuck*:

> Yeah, but like—I could never just walk up to a strange chick on the street, ever—and the guys who can go by them in cars and hang out the window and go, "Whaddya say, baby?" I mean they just *amaze* me—and I think like, the reason for that is, well O.K., my mother and my aunt—every day they came home with stories about some guy who was behind the bushes exposing himself. And, well it's really hung me up. Like, O.K., dig—they wanted me to believe that there was a band of dedicated perverts who spent their whole lives in trick positions waiting for them to come out of the BMT.
> "O.K. guys, oil up your zippers—it's five o'clock. Lenny Bruce's mother and aunt are due any minute now. You take the elevator, you take the bus, I got the subway."

And figure—then he turns himself into the whole crew of them. The intrepid flashers ready to pounce his

31

yiddisha Aunt Mema who forever stalked the city with a pocketbook big enough to double as a deadly weapon. This woman who saw lust lurking behind every turnstile, every casual brush of every corduroy shoulderpad.

"Hey lady, this way—over here, lady—in the bushes . . ." Find the *shmuck* in the bush! That's all they got to do all day, right? Waiting around for Mema to get them with that big black pocketbook, with that scream of hers—
"Feh! Feh!" (laughing at his own imitation)
The Jewish seagull: "Feh! Feh!"
I mean it—that's why I can never talk to a strange chick on the street.

CHAPTER 7

HONEY BRUCE RAN HER HAND THROUGH HER STRAGGLY hair. The thought crossed her mind that she ought to wash it. She would. Sure. When she got a chance.

The interviewer asked her again about what happened next. O.K., she met Lenny. It was love at first fuck. Then what?

"Then? Let's see—Then?"

"Did you stay together? Right from the start?"

"Well no—Oh yeah. See, I had to go to Miami. I had this job? But Lenny called me every day. And then one day he called and said he just couldn't stand to be without me. You know?

"Well, see, I was working in a club in South Beach and I lived at the *Floridian*. He'd call and he'd say why couldn't I find a nearer place? It was a *shlep* and all. He was really you know, concerned, and all. And then—well—well—"

Three-fifteen and quiet. Honey'd gotten out of the club ten minutes early and still had the tassels attached to her nipples under her sarong dress. She jumped into her white '49 Chevy convertible and sank into the leopard upholstery as tired as Mrs. Wirtzchafter across town at Acme Insurance after four hours of scrubbing floors.

It might say "Hot" Harlow on the side of her car. She might look dime in her G-string, but six days a week, three shows a night of rolling it around up there wears you out even at twenty-four.

She drove through the deadbeat streets one light after another. Not a car. Not a trolley shaking. Just Honey and the night, the palms and Miami. *Surfside, Beach Haven, Coconut Grove.* And, Honey, Honey, Honey, that's all Lenny could think of. He swore to her. He wrote. He promised. Every day another letter. Together they would find the good life, a better agent and a double billing somewhere where they should live and be well, happily ever after. All of which was Jake with Honey—that wacked-up nut—as she dragged ass to her room.

"29C, please."

But wacked-up wasn't half strong enough to describe that maniac as she opened her door and then stood in the doorway shell-shocked. A letter she'd anticipated—O.K., a telegram—but 457 #6 potato chip cans stuffed with gladioli? Millions and tons of pink and orange day-old bargain gladioli as far as the mind could boggle? On the vanity, on the bed, against four walls—gladioli everywhere with that treacle MGM jungle reek? "Sweet Jesus," she murmured, "wacked-up doesn't begin to call it."

"Oh you maniac screwball," she sighed, sinking down on the faded satin chaise. "You beautiful maniac screwball, where the hell are you?" and then found the note on the mirror, which read,

"I love you. The Guy in 34B."

"Ohmygod"—dialing the desk—

34

"Operator?" Why doesn't she answer? "Operator? 34B, please, and hurry," all the time getting out of her Dorothy Lamour, spitting on the mirror to clear a spot so she could fix herself up, so she could—

"Beauty Parlor," the voice in 34B answered: "Leg waxing, underarm hickies and crossed eyes straightened."

"Oh baby, it's—it's paradise."

"You knew it was me?"

"In potato chip cans?"

"I'll be right up."

"Give me five minutes."

"You, a headliner? You can't strip in less than five minutes?"

"Lenny?"

Only he was already out the door. Already bebopping down the hallway, into the stairwell and down the banister. He couldn't have put into any kind of words, why she was so, well, special. Sure the looks, the legs, the skin like Madame Chiang Kai-shek sheets, but more—Something bigger than special, as he raced, skittered and banged into her door, opened it and saw her, arms up against the wall surrounded by the flowers. Busby Berkley in 3D.

126 pounds of Maraschino cherries and all his.

CHAPTER 8

A DOLL HE CAN CARRY.

Peg of His Heart.

Just like the girl that married the dear old dad off a *Saturday Evening Post* cover.

Monday he took her to see the Dade County Court House and bought her a Nedicks.

Tuesday it was six hours of surf fishing with a bent pin and a piece of kite string.

Wednesday they did Carnival Town, Miami Beach's answer to the Cote D'Azur. They saw joints, *yentas* and off-the-shoulder cashmere undershirts for three hundred bucks wholesale.

They did dancing. They did numbers. They stayed in bed in 37 different positions for eleven hours a day. Eight months in six days they did. Hot Honey and Hungry Lenny.

Then Artie called. Artie was Lenny's buddy. He did things for Lenny. He was always around, you never knew when there were pieces to piece together. Artie told Lenny on the phone he ought to do himself a favor and deep-six Honey. That she wasn't for him he said—that she was trouble.

"By the time she was fifteen she'd already done time, Lenny, so you can imagine—Look, Lenny, you and me we go back to jerking off in the alley. Would I give you a bum rap, baby? Would I steer you wrong?"

"She did what? She— Hey, what did you do for your old buddy, Art. Did you hire a private eye on her?"

"What private eye? Look Lenny. Remember when I saw her in Baltimore I said, 'I think I know her from somewhere'? Well, I remembered, that's all, so O.K., I like you, I—Look, even though it's none of my business, I asked around, that's all. I started hearing things, and I—Hey, look man. I don't have to spell it out for you, do I?"

"Listen Artie, you don't have to—"

"Now don't go getting sore on me. I just hate to see you make a *shmuck* out of yourself, that's all."

"Sure, sure—buddy. Yeah. My Mother, ah, she didn't have anything to do with your putting the ear to the grapevine did she?"

"Sally?"

"Yeah. Yeah, Sally."

"Look Lenny. I'm not making this stuff up. You don't believe me, go check it out yourself."

"I don't have to check shit. She already told me herself. But you can tell my old lady from me that the next time she wants to hire a John Alden to come on strong for her tell her to hire Charlie McCarthy. He does a smoother job."

"Who was that, baby?" Honey asked him after he hung up.

"Yeah?"

"On the phone—who was it?"

"You know something," Lenny says, taking that face of hers in his hand.

"What?"

"Let's get married, baby. That's what."

CHAPTER 9

"WELL SO WE GOT MARRIED. IN, UH—YEAH, THE SPRING of 1951."

She laughs, but it's hard. Her eyes go suddenly weak. 1951? Has it been that long? Her whole lifetime ago?

"Yeah, I was a lovely bride—and, uh—yeah, I had on white shoes, a little suit. The judge was Judge Hunt, I even remember his name. That's funny, huh? 1951 and I still remember the guy's name."

"And then you went to meet Sally, and Lenny's aunt?"

"Yeah. Then I went to meet the family."

"Look Mema, what's done is done. He married her. He's bringing her home. So what's the good of carrying on. We'll have a meal and you'll see. The roof won't fall in and the sky won't fall down either."

"In jail she was? Lenny's girl was in jail?"

"Not his girl, Mema. His wife. So what's the difference already if she was in jail. A lot of kids, they're young, they take a ride in a car that doesn't belong to them—it happens. And she's Lenny's wife. We're going to treat her like a perfect lady and you'll see. She'll be a perfect lady. What are they doing?"

"Doing? I'm looking—I'm looking and they're sitting. He sits in the driver's seat and she, she sits there, one cigarette after another. He doesn't get up. She doesn't get up. They're going to sit there all day, Sadie? The pot roast, it'll get burned."

The ex-Sadie Kitchenberg gets up and walks to her sister's window to see for herself. On the way she passes the mirror and takes a quick satisfied peek. O.K., here, with Mema, she'd always be Sadie, but who could look at that Oomph girl and think of anybody but a Sally. Sally on Shubert Alley—

Mema was right. They *were* just sitting there. Sally watched them; her son and his bride. So why didn't they come up? Lenny ought to know her better than that. O.K., she tried. If she could have found a way to break them up, she would have. You don't kick your heels when your only son goes and marries himself that kind of trouble. Still—

"She's probably a very lovely girl," she said. She gave her hairdo another primp and turned to Mema. "Let's give her a chance. If Lenny likes her. If she makes him happy."

"Mmmmmm," Mema said, half agreeing and half tasting the carrots.

They were going to have a ruined supper if they didn't stop sitting downstairs so long in the car, that's what was on Mema's mind.

"By me, I'm wondering what can they have to talk about so long?" She came over and sat by her sister. "Already they're married a week. Why don't they come upstairs, they can sit here. We can eat. *Nu*—if they want to do so much talking, who's stopping them? Let them talk here."

Except that downstairs in the Chevy it wasn't just a question of talking. Honey was scared. She'd already rolled, smoked and finished one joint and was working on her second.

"Just give me another second," she said and took a long compulsive pull, which drove Lenny bananas. It was O.K. in a room. It was O.K. in a head somewhere—but out there on the street where anybody can walk by, who knows what's moving? You had to use a little discretion.

"O.K., O.K.," he said looking around. "But put the joint out, will ya man? You're really getting to me."

"I'm nervous," she says, taking another hit and passing it to him.

She wasn't the only one. He starts to put out the evidence, but can't resist. At the last minute he takes a drag himself and then snuffs it, saving the roach. He puts this last bit in his sock and smiles at Honey primping in the rearview mirror.

"Look, it's not gonna be a bad scene. First of all, my mother'll be 'on' all the time. Shit—she won't even know you're there. And my Aunt Mema—You're gonna split a gut. I'll get her to say 'feh' for you, you'll love her."

"Yeah, I know, I know. I'm gonna love her."

"So O.K., man—let's go."

"All right, we'll go. But, hey, Lenny, will you do me a favor? Will you quit calling me 'man'?"

CHAPTER 10

HOW RIGHT LENNY WAS. IT WAS TERRIFIC. THE PLACE, the food. Honey, in her life, had never tasted such pot roast. And she was just high enough. The way Sally looked at her. The way Mema stared. After a while she just kind of forgot about it, especially after Sally started on her routines. That's one thing about Lenny. He certainly knew his old lady.

From two minutes after the coffee, Sally was off. She did the "you shoulda seen Lenny when we brought him home from the hospital" number. From there to the one about him peeing his pants on the subway and sitting in it all the way from DeKalb to Avenue U.

"Oh, I gotta tell ya about the first time this *shmuck* here ever worked in a club."

She was all over him, her Lenny. She was squeezing him, messing around in his hair, pinching his cheeks. As if she was up for the American-Mother-of-the-Year Award.

"Sit down Sally," Lenny said, laughing and giving Honey the "didn't I tell you?" look.

"You've been 'on' for two hours already."

Sally, she never even skipped a beat. "So," she said, "he'd never been on stage before, ever—and I was working this club on Ocean Parkway."

"*The Victory Club.*"

"Right. Boy was it a joint."

"Joint? Hell, the owner was a guy—"

"Hey! Sonny boy! Who's doin' the bit, you or me?"

Not that she wouldn't cut off her arm for him. Look, there was nothing she wouldn't do for her Lenny, but lay off already, a bit was a bit.

"Sure," Lenny said, beaming. Was she terrific, that mother of his? Terrific?

"See—so the customers were guys who were so tough—so tough, they wore wool suits in the summer. Right?"

"You forgot, with no underwear."

"Yeah—Yeah." And they were laughing. Sally was up "doing" everybody, Honey was plain happy and even Mema would forget every so often to stare at the *shiksa* . . . that *coorvah* Lenny had found in some gutter somewhere.

"O.K. With no underwear. So—anyway, one night the MC, he doesn't show. He has a little trouble with his car. The bulls found a little pot in the trunk."

Lenny breaks up.

She turns to Honey, shaking her head. "Willya listen to that cackle on him. I'll telling you I'm the only person can make that Lenny of mine belly-yuk. If you think it's easy, try it. That one—wheew. O.K., so where was I? Yeah, so I'm sitting at the bar and I'm—"

"Tell me," Mema suddenly interrupts. She's facing Honey.

"Tell me, Miss. How long you and Leonard, you knew each other before you got married?"

"Hey—hey, Mema . . . I'm 'on,' O.K.?"

"O.K., O.K.," Mema says with her eyes, "I was only

42

asking." To which Sally's eyes say, "Well have a little consideration," and she's back on track.

"So. There I am, right? I'm sitting at the bar and it's showtime. And there's no MC. And who should walk in? I'm tellin' you—I turn around and there he is, Lenny. Could I die?"

Honey's watching them, the mother and the son. They're so much alike it's wild. She starts the sentence, he finishes it. The same delivery, the same memories. They go back a long time, those two—and not just in the ordinary kid-mama way. They're really into the same bag, like Martin and Lewis or something.

Lenny's tugging on Honey's sleeve. He wants to explain something so she can really get the picture.

"You gotta see what I was wearing, baby. You know those brown suede dude shoes, the shirt with the Billy Eckstine collar, and the handkerchief with the five points?"

"With the sticker still on": Sally. And then back to Lenny.

"Made in the Philippines," and back to Sally.

"Yeah, made in the Philippines. So anyway, I says, 'Lenny, there's no MC; how about if I introduce you and then you can introduce the acts?' He says, 'Are you kiddin' with that?' I says, 'It's a big nothing. You don't have to be funny, just—you know, straight intros: And now, folks, here's *Schmutz* and *Dreck,* let's have a big hand. Yeah? O.K.?' So he says, 'O.K.' Right? O.K.! So it gets to be fifteen minutes to showtime and I'm lookin' all over the club. No Lenny. Then it gets to be *ten* minutes to showtime—"

Lenny taps Honey on the shoulder.

"I'm in the toilet," he says, "puking my guts out—all over my brown suede shoes I'm puking."

He's laughing.

Honey's thrown her arms around him, "Oh, my poor little baby—"

And it's Mema's turn again. "Lenny?" she says in a very serious voice, but nobody has time for Mema now. Sally's still "on."

"Sure," says Sally, "it's O.K. with him. He's out there puking all over his shoes, but what about me? I'm the one up front with the restless natives. One joke, another joke, I don't know whether to what—and then there he is: Lenny, looking like the cocker spaniel that got its ears caught in the Bendix. But it's now or never, right?"

"Right": Honey, she pecks Lenny on his nose.

"Sure right, so I'm off: folks, I say, the MC couldn't make it tonight, blah blah blah—but luckily, a *good* friend of mine and a funny funny guy—"

"What do you mean funny? You said, '*the funniest* guy in the world—' "

"Yeah, right—Mister Leonard Alfred Schneider, who just flew in from the coast to do the Sullivan Show, happens to be in the club—and here he is folks—"

"You hip to what she's done to me, that dumb broad?" shaking his head, gesturing for his wife to take a gander at that mother of his. "She's got the band going big, the lights picking me out like lint on a blue suit. Hell, I'd never even been up on a stage before, not even at Assembly at P.S. Hoo Hah, and now—now I gotta go out there and be the funniest guy in the world?"

The tears are running down Sally's face.

"Wait," she screams, getting up in her beaded black to take Center Stage again. "Oh God, you shoulda seen him! He was so nervous, he rushes out like the whole precinct's chasing him and right away, oh God—" She's laughing so hard she can hardly continue: "right away he trips over the light cord and throws us both—flat on our asses—God!" She's crying and the tears are streaking her mascara down her cheeks like Glen plaid.

"God, that was funny, Lenny, tell the truth—was that funny?"

"Some funny," except he's doubled up too. Sally, Lenny and Honey can't get over it. Sally thinking about the expression on Lenny's face. Lenny remembering the brown suede shoes and Honey loving the center of the inner circle. Everybody's having a ball. Everybody but Mema. Mema is only waiting they should stop already with the uproar. Mema wants answers.

"So—*nu? Nu,* Lenny?" she asks and he finally turns around.

"What, Memshka—What is it?"

"The same what it was before. You'll tell me please how long you two lovebirds knew each other before already you're married?"

"How long?"

"That's right. I would like to know."

"About a half an hour."

"Hey, comeon Lenny—" Honey was trying to make a good impression.

"I picked her up on an empty car on the D Train. Gave her the old MGM smile and—" he snaps his fingers for Honey's corroboration.

"Right, baby?"

"Feh! Lenny—feh!" Mema says. About some things even *he* has to be serious.

Never mind, Lenny's day is made.

"Did I tell you I could get her to do the 'feh?' My own Jewish seagull! Do you know how many flashers she's deafened with that 'feh' of hers?"

He looks around at the women in his life and figures even with the "feh's" he has it pretty cushy.

CHAPTER 11

ON THE WAY HOME LENNY CAN'T KEEP HIS HANDS OFF her. Getting across Flatbush Avenue Extension, Manhattan Bridge and Canal Street are too much for him. He wants her instantly.

And even, later, when he's got her. When he's lying on his back rubbing his mind on the inside of her thighs as she slowly and knowingly takes everything off just for him.

First the little white blouse she bought just for Mema.

The skirt.

The slip.

As she stops to step up on the bed, one leg under his right armpit, the other on his left thigh. As she slowly pivots and rolls her hips back again even slower.

He's dying. He feels like he's in a steam bath. He's groaning, as she runs her hands over her breasts. As she rubs them back again, as she finally leans over his face to give him a taste.

This Honey—this wife, this cross between the kindergarten teacher and the $500-a-night hooker. Nobody ought to have it so heavy.

It ought to be at least fattening.

And they start moving West—

Honey's working Detroit.

The guys are pelting her with fivers as she grinds away for them and across the border in Ontario, Lenny's headlining at the *Elmwood*. It's a class club. He's beginning, he's beginning. And almost instantly, he don't want his personal stuff, she shouldn't oughta be up there throwing it around for the slobs anymore. He don't like it, that's all, do him something—he just don't like it.

There's no bigger test of how hip you really are than when your girlfriend becomes your wife—dig what I mean? O.K., you talk to the average Joe:

"Ain't that a pretty chick?"

"Yeah. She's beautiful—got a real pretty face—nutty jugs—"

"Well, would you marry a woman like that?"

"You kiddin' me? Sure, I'd marry her."

"Well, would you let your wife dress that way?"

"You kiddin' me? I'd bust her ass."

"Well, what did you dig her for in the first place?"

" 'Cause her jugs were stickin' out—"

"But you don't want her to dress that way now?"

"You crazy or somethin'? She's my wife!"

Yeah?

Yeah.

Just like what happened with Lenny and Honey. Right after she stripped for him personally, that was it for him.

"O.K., O.K. I admit it. It bugs the hell outa me. With your boobs, your *pupick* stickin' out there—those bullyacks creamin' all over you, with their newspapers in their laps. It drives me nuts, baby. Drives me absofuckinglutely nuts."

"You're jealous."

"O.K., so I'm jealous."

"But I thought—I mean I thought we agreed, you know, I'd work, we'd—"

"I changed my mind."

"You are, Lenny, I can't believe it. You're really jealous."

"All right already, what is it, some kind of miracle?"

"You know, I like that."

"You don't mind?"

"No man I like it, but what'll I do? Baby—I mean what else do I know besides stripping?"

"I got it all figured out. You'll sing. It'll go—you'll see. We'll do a double."

"I got a picture of that: you'll strip and I'll tell mother-in-law jokes. Whatd'ya mean, double?"

"I'm telling you. You'll sing. You'll be terrific."

"Lenny, I can't sing a note. In school I was practically a listener."

"Comeon, baby, you can sing as well as anybody. Look at you. With your stuff? Honey, I'll teach you. In six weeks we'll have you signed up with the *Metropolitan*."

"Who do you think you are, Flo Ziegfeld?"

"I think I'm your husband, baby, and do me something—I don't want you out there with those bastards eating up what's mine. My *goyisha punim*. Let'm go out and get their own."

CHAPTER 12

SO YEAH, HE STARTED WORKING WITH ME. YOU KNOW, to be a singer? And he really played like he was Flo Ziegfield or somebody. I had to do exercises. No kidding. He'd listen to me and—well, it was fun. We were together, you know—24 hours a day."

The interviewer s been looking at this woman. He's figuring if she was married in '51—Could she be that old? It doesn't figure. She didn't say how old she was when she and Lenny got married. He better not ask. O.K., she's a little banged up, who wouldn't be the way they lived it up and down, but neither would he kick her out of bed.

"So, then we started working around. Yeah, club dates, the Catskills—it wasn't a bad act."

You ever been to the Catskills on one of those big fall weekends? The smell of prime ribs, lox and napoleons smothered in seven-layer cake? The voices of pharmacists and their platinum-haired women. The eleven-year-old daughters who already have a weight problem. The Social Director who's getting laryngitis from telling all the divorcees he'll meet them later.

"Now hear this—Now hear this—" The PA system announcing the table-tennis tournament. Announcing coffee with forty-three kinds pastry being served in the lower level dining room. Announcing Lenny and Honey Bruce, that funny funny man and the singer with the gold tonsils in the after hours club.

It's a good gig. You eat well. You loll around by the indoor pool and pretty soon, if you've got a wife who looks as good as Honey, Sherman Hart'll come by. He'll sit down. Next to Honey of course, in her lap if he could get away with it, and he'll throw his weight around, which is plenty in this business. A guy like Sherman Hart is nobody to sneeze at. He'll give you a little advice and you, if you're smart, you'll keep your yap shut, Lenny, you'll take his advice and later you can paper the walls with it.

"Not a bad act, kid—not bad. You've got a clever husband there, young lady. He's a real comer."

"You've got good taste, Mr. Sherman," she says, because everybody knows Mister Entertainment Hart likes a woman with at least a few wits about her.

"And that's a very pretty little lady you got there," he says to Lenny, his eyes boring through Honey's bra.

"Thank you," she says, giving Lenny a look. Don't screw up. Don't say a word—a bastard like Hart can kill you in these hills, Lenny. And these hills is where it's at for us, where you get a hold on the big enchiladas.

"Uh huh," he says. "Very pretty."

"I might even be able to use you on my show sometime." And then with precision timing, he turns to Lenny: "Cause I love ya, Lenny—I love you younger guys coming up. You younger guys are what makes this business such a pleasure for me." His hand on Honey's thigh. "Who the hell wants to be a parent with no children, a king with no princes—"

Jesus, can this guy lay it on.

"Talking to Henny Youngman just the other night on the Barry Gray Show about that—"

The guy's really incredible.

"By the way," he says, seeing an opportunity to feast his fangs on Honey again. "You happen to catch the show?"

"She never misses it, Sherman. Do you, doll?"

"Never," she says, looking into Hart's eyes and digging her nails into Lenny's wrist.

"Anyway kiddo, what I mean is—you're so talented, I mean I'd hate to see you get off on the worng foot. Work clean, Lenny. With your talent, you don't need to come on with the filth."

Lenny has dropped his eyes and begins to shuffle his foot back and forth, the way a kid does when he's caught with his hands in his mother's brassiere drawer. He's got that altar boy look in his eyes. Eighteen-carat repentance.

"Because, you know, there were a few beefs about your show the other night and lucky for you I ran into Jack Goldstein and I kept him from phoning in a bad report on you."

By this time Hart is shaking his head and almost wagging his finger under Lenny's chin. Lenny comes in with the chorus.

"That was really white of you, Sherm, but it was a mistake, man. A comedy of errors and all. One of those nights, you know. I was bored. Every night the same old Becky and Jakes—and it was hot, so—like, I took off my jacket, and I turned to the band and said, 'O.K., now for my jacket off bit—' And the mike picked it up, and well, the guys in the band cracked up and I caught Honey's eye in the wings—"

"Yeah, and I cracked up—"

"So then I cracked up. And it got well, man, it just took off. It looked really funky, Sherm, but it was just—"

And Honey's dying. That Lenny. He really knows

how to lay it on. She looks away so the big bastard won't see her doubling up. On the other side of the pool, she sees four ladies in bathing suits with skirts. They're playing Canasta with eight rings and twelve pounds of engorged veins on each hand.

She also sees Jack Goldstein, the owner, the live-and-be-well backslapper who, spotting Lenny and Hart, gives the drop dead to a couple of nobody guests and comes over, to add his nickel.

"So? Sherman? Did you tell him?"

"You got yourself a winner, Jack. A real comer. We talked, we got along and don't worry—I think we got a couple things ironed out, didn't we kid?"

"Terrific. He's got a good boy, a good boy. Nuts! But the audience loves him. Booked his mother—funny lady that Sally—And—" Here Goldstein leaned over and gave Lenny a big wink.

"She works clean, your mother. Like a whistle."

Goldstein's happy. The wink's not enough for him. He leans forward again and taking Lenny's face between his thumb and forefinger gives it such a squeeze—shaking it back and forth, forth and back.

"So, *meshugeneh*—did my friend, Sherm, straighten you out a little?" Still shaking and still squeezing, till Lenny pulls back and rubs his aching jaw.

"You know that's why Jewish boys all end up going to the orthodontist."

He looks at Goldstein. Goldstein shakes his head before cracking up. Honey cracks up. Lenny even gives a little laugh, and then finally, Sherman Hart raises one finger in the air, as if to pass judgment from the throne, and says,

"Now *that's* funny."

Lenny's been baptized. And on that pontifical note, the two men get up to go, but not before Sherman points out a young yum yum to Goldstein.

"That one—how old is she?"

Goldstein, giving Lenny the A.O.K. sign over his

52

shoulder, thinks a minute. "Going on seventeen, give or take—"

"Yeah?"

Hart gives the *zahftik* young miss another going-over with his eyes.

"So, I'll take— Get her for me," he says to Goldstein, smiles at the girl, and walks slowly away, blowing thoughtfully on his nails.

CHAPTER 13

THE SPOT'S ON HONEY, IN HER $17.95 OFF-THE-SHOUL-
der from Klein's on the Square. The original million-
dollar *shiksa* from the five-and-ten-cent dream, and
what's the difference if she's no Lily Pons *kinehurrah,*
she can at least carry a tune.

She sings her last song and it's Lenny's turn.

"Is that a winner chick?" he asks them and they're
clapping so hard, these Seventh-Avenue *shlockers* away
for four days fun they almost miss his: "Is that the
most *goyish goyish?*".

They start laughing. Nothing a Jewish audience
likes better than downing its own.

"You want to know from *goyish?*" Again he points
towards Honey, who turns a little back and forth
everybody shouldn't miss a thing.

"O.K. *shiksas—*" and they're still looking. These
cloak-and-suiters. What? From *shiksas—this* punk kid
is gonna tell *them?*

"And it's not that Jewish chicks are lushes, you

54

know, but comeon—that pink-nippled, freckled *goyisha punim!* This is *hais,* boy, that is a rare tribe. O.K., take Elizabeth Taylor—even if I can't *sèe* the mustache, I know she's got it. That's all. It's enough. And a mole with the hair on it. It's just a cooking thing the pharaohs have. O.K.?"

Sure, O.K., they laugh—even though the old lady and the small fat one are looking at them like, what? Allavasudden, we're not good enough no more? Allavasudden, we're not *goyish?* But they're clapping anyway. And they're laughing till the tears come, and then Lenny comes on with his serious look.

There's Sherman Hart up front with the little number from poolside that afternoon. Lenny looks around; he stops his *shtick,* he's gonna do a little PR here, play the old showbiz soft-shoe softsoap:

"I wanna tell you you're wonderful, folks, you're really wonderful. Now for any of you who don't know, I wanna tell you that right here tonight, sitting right down there—is one of the all-time greats of this business—"

The lights pick Hart out and he gives everybody the famous teeth for a minute, knowing that Lenny's only started. He has plenty of time to get up, and really let them get a look at him.

"A man who got his start right here in this hotel— 'Mister Entertainment' himself: Sherman Hart! Ladies and gentlemen—let's really let him know what we think of him—Sherman Hart!" And Lenny's making with the gestures. He wants a big hand. He gets it. And now it's Sherman's cue. He's up. He gives them the old humble bow routine. He blows a few kisses.

"Thank you very much, Lenny—I love you—Ladies and Gentlemen—Lenny, I wanna tell you, I love everything you're doing up there—and you're gonna love it too—" (He moves away from the table just a hair so the girl with him doesn't come in for any of the spotlight.)

"You're gonna love it when you see it again next Wednesday night on my new Comedy Hour on CBS. That's nine P.M. Eastern Standard Time, Seven P.M. Rocky Mountain Time, and Four A.M. in Tokyo."

The laugh is there. Again he gives them the horse-teeth.

"So talk a little slower, willya Lenny? I can't write that fast."

And everybody's having a ball. They know he's teasing. He wouldn't do that to a nice guy like Lenny Bruce. Lenny Bruce is having a ball, look at him laughing it up, and why not, Sherman Hart's the biggest. He should be so big.

"*Sherman Hart,* ladies and gentlemen." Again Lenny leads on applause.

But happiest of all is Jack Goldstein. He's standing in the back looking over all he surveys and owns. He knows that when everybody's happy, he gets rich.

"You know folks," he hears Lenny say with that ring of truth only those showbiz guys know how to get:

"I'm a little new to this business and—I know I still have a lot to learn."

"Attaboy, Lenny, you're gonna go far. You're a *mensch* Lenny, a chip off the old Sally."

"I have a lot to learn and thanks to Sherman Hart I realize I made a mistake out here the other night."

Sherman looks up and throws Lenny the three rings: "I'm with you, baby."

"And if I offended any of you, I'd really like to apologize. So. By way of making it up to you I, ah—I think—I think I'm gonna piss on you," and he goes for his zipper.

"He's gonna what?" Goldstein mutters to a passing waiter. "He's what?"

"That's it, baby," the waiter mutters, moving by with a trayful of boiled beef thermidor.

And twenty minutes later, Honey and Lenny are on their way. It's pouring. They're throwing their things into the Chevy. Goldstein's standing there with *The News* over his head, dying from them.

"Why? You can't tell a person why? Who talks such things, Lenny? I never heard such a—"

He just wants an explanation, that's all. O.K., he lost his act, so he'll call MCA, there are plenty of guys who'll come out by the six o'clock. That's not the point. The point is what is it with this *meshugeneh?*

"Was I ever anything but kind? What did I do, I wasn't generous? Tell me, I wanna know. Why would a person do such a thing? Especially on a High Holy Day weekend?" But he might as well go orate to the badminton rackets. Honey's getting in the car and Lenny hands her their music.

Goldstein comes around and stands in Lenny's way.

"Look man, I just wanna get out of this hell-hole, O.K.?"

He goes around to shut the trunk. Goldstein's after him. And all of a sudden, it's no more Mr. Nice Guy.

"Believe me, *kanacker*—you're such a *kanacker?* From this you're not going to hear the end. You'll never play another resort. A club. A room. From nobody will you get a date. You're finished, *kanacker*, you can't talk like a person. I'm telling you it's over for you, show business."

Lenny just gets in the driver's seat and rolls down the window.

"I'm shittin' sheckels, man."

"Tough guy. O.K., watch, tough guy—you got a rough road ahead of you. A rough road."

Lenny pulls away from the drive. Goldstein shouts after him.

"Especially with your *no-talent* wife! Especially!"

Honey stiffens. It's as if they've both been zinged by the same arrow. Lenny stops the car, backs it up and rolls down the window. Then, pinning Goldstein between the eyes, he leans out and says with quiet intensity:

"You know, Goldstein—there's not one Puerto Rican in your kitchen that hasn't *shtupped* your wife."
Game One.
Decision: Lenny Bruce?

CHAPTER 14

"MY GOD, BABY," HONEY CRIED, WINCING. WITH THE rain out there, and the way Lenny was taking those curves, it looked like they were going to sideswipe that tree.

Up the road about twelve miles, a hunter in a bright orange jacket said the same thing to his buddy, who was wearing a black and red mackinaw.

"Forcrissakes, Charlie, take it easy, willya? What are you tryin' to do, kill us?"

It was some rain.

Charlie had taken the station wagon and was pissed off that Eddie was the only one of the four of them who had gotten his deer. The same thing last year. The four of them go out, Eddie comes home with the only bacon. It's enough to make you chew nails or something.

It's getting late. Everybody's hungry. The smell of wet wool permeates the air of the station wagon. Wet wool, sweat and a half empty bottle of *Cutty Sark.*

"What time will we get in?" Honey says.

Lenny says, "Yeah."

The windshield wiper's playing upyours, upyours, upyours, in front of his eyes and the damn road keeps disappearing right the hell out from under him.

"Is that a restaurant? Up there—on the left?"

But Lenny doesn't have time for restaurants. He's moving along through the rain and watching out for what's coming in between figuring a new act. A new comeon—something—

"I'm getting hungry, Lenny. Lenny?"

But Lenny doesn't answer her. He swerves. The station wagon swerves, but it's too slippery. The brakes are wet or the tires don't have any traction, or the road has gone fishing. Anyway, it's terrible. One moment of realization what's coming and then a splintering of endless glass. The strange sound of bodies and steel breaking apart with the same impact. Screams and desperation and horror.

Lenny's jacknifed into the station wagon and the station wagon has jacknifed into Lenny.

Mostly there's just blood. Some of it the deer's, some of it theirs. Mostly Honey's. Lenny's all right.

He picks himself up. The hood of the station wagon. . . The rear legs of the deer are lying on Honey. He tears himself out from behind the steering wheel. He's wild with terror.

"Honey!" he's screaming, "Honey, Honey—Oh my God, my Honey."

She's covered with sheet music. She's lying worse than dead and all the time he holds her in his arms the blood pours from her face, her arms, her body. He can't look. He feels her. He holds her but to see how parts of her no longer fit where they're supposed to, he can't. He's crying too much. Praying to God too hard.

"Don't die," he begs. He promises God he'll never, never again do anything. He'll be good. He'll be anything.

"Please dear God, don't let her die. Please God—please."

CHAPTER 15

THE BUSTLE OF ACTIVITY IN THE INTENSIVE CARE WARD is at a distance. Where Lenny sits with that vacant stare around his eyes, it's pretty quiet. Some kid's mother sits in a corner crying steadily. Another one of her kids hangs around trying to amuse himself with the light cord. Lenny looks at them absently. Whenever there's a sound from down the hall, he jumps up. The good-looking well-off local housewife who does volunteer work at the desk shakes her head, and he sits down again.

She brings him a cup of coffee, and, God help him, he knows, with his black eye and his arm in a sling, he's watching that porch swing of hers as she comes towards him. Still he's only noticing, he tells himself. She's the one who's swinging it.

"Thanks," he says and she smiles. She goes back to her desk and knows the same score he does. They have both played out the same scene a million times before—except that this time Honey lies in the other room close to death.

Her bladder has been punctured. She's in shock. Her beautiful *punim* is so badly beat up, who knows whether he'll ever recognize her again.

The phone on the nurse's aide's desk rings. Everybody in the waiting room looks up. The mother knows it isn't for her. But she looks up anyway. It'll never be for her. She knows that too.

"Yes, I will," the nurse's aide says and then turns towards Lenny.

"Mr. Bruce?"

He follows her. His eyes go blank. As he walks down the hall, through the double doors, past a doctor and past a widow of two minutes he's barely conscious. He looks away from the aide. He looks at the machinery working around the clock all around him. Everywhere people are plugged into something, in the hope that the twentieth century is going to keep them alive a little longer. He walks and he looks but he's just barely keeping himself together.

It's so quiet in Honey's room. His face tenses. A curtain has been pulled in one half of the room. Somebody is behind it sobbing. Somebody else is saying a Hail Mary. He can hear a rustling of sheets.

And then he sees Honey.

At least he thinks it's Honey.

Her face is a mess of swollen bruises and stitched wounds. The only identifying feature on her is her beautiful red hair, stained with blood, stinking with vomit. Her eyes are open as if she sees him, but she's only barely there. He looks down and touches her bed with the tips of his fingers. He opens his mouth and then closes it. What can he say? What would he say if he could?

After a moment the sound of officious starch introduces a nurse who comes in on cuban heels, her hair in a net. Without a word to Lenny, she rolls up Honey's sleeve and prepares to give her a shot of morphine.

Lenny can't help himself. He smiles.

"Some people have all the fun," he says.

The nurse doesn't think he's funny.

Well, neither does he. He gets the hell out of there. He goes down the hall and punches the *Down* button on the elevator. Then he hears his name called and turns. .

"Mr. Bruce?" he hears and something clicks.

"Yes?"

It's nice ass, with his raincoat over her arm.

"You forgot something," she says and again that smile.

"Oh," he says, looking around quickly to size up the possibilities. "Thank you very much."

"You're welcome," and she's on her way back to her desk. But not before passing the telephone booths, the two of them, where, if nobody was coming, and he was standing in front of her with his raincoat on and they were very fast about it. . . Forget it— telephone booths are not this lady's style. Later they'll check into some classy room someplace. There'll be sheets, a down comforter on the bed. She'll have pink panties with rosebuds on them. And it won't be as good as with Honey. But never mind. It'll be something.

CHAPTER 16

Let's face it—guys are different. And ladies just don't understand this, so—ladies are one emotion and guys detach. They don't consciously detach, but they do detach. Now a lady can't fall through a plate glass window and go to bed with you ten seconds later. Ugh ughh. When they don't feel good, they don't feel good, but every guy in this audience is the same. You can just idolize your wife, be so crazy about her— Be on your way home from work, have a head-on collision with a Greyhound bus—forty people lying dead on the highway—and in the ambulance the guy makes a play for the nurse.

WIFE: How could you do a thing like that?
GUY: I got horny.
WIFE: You got what?
GUY: I got hot.
WIFE: How could you get hot with your foot cut off? People were bleeding to death and dying.
GUY: I dunno. I just got hot.

WIFE: He's an animal, that one. He got hot with his foot cut off.

GUY: I guess I'm an animal. I dunno.

WIFE: What did you get hot at?

GUY: The nurse's uniform, I think.

LENNY: Yeah. See, it has nothing to do with liking, loving. Guys detach. You can put a guy on a desert island and he'll do it to mud—a barrel—a chicken. So, if you came home and found your husband sitting on the bed with a chicken—would that be the end of your marriage?

HER, again: A chicken!!! A chicken in our bed.

HIM: Lemme alone. That's all.

HER: Don't touch me! You want your dinner, get your chicken to get it for you!

LENNY: See, in New York it's illegal—"seeming sexual intercourse with a chicken." That's the literal—but how could you even fantasize that, doing it to a chicken? They're too short. How could you kiss a chicken—with that dopey face?

HER: How come you're alone tonight? Your chicken left town?

HIM: I dunno the chicken. I was drunk. I met her in the yard. Whaddya want from me? Stop already with the chicken.

He has to give them a minute to keep from choking. He gives them a look and then he moves:

You know whenever I cheat on my wife I always tell her. I'm just that kind of a husband. I just, if I cheat on her, I just, I just gotta be truthful, I can't lie, and I always tell her.

THE VOICE OF REASON: Never tell her. Not if you love your wife.

HUSBAND: I just can't help it. I'm honest and when I chippy on her I just *gotta* tell her—cause I like to *Hurt* her:

"Ah, sweetheart, ah, you didn't find this handkerchief with lipstick on it and I wanna show it to ya. I wanna confess. Ah, I cheated on ya again, and, ah, I always wanna tell you when I cheat on ya, cause I know that you should leave me—and take the eight kids with ya. I wouldn't blame ya. And if ya had a job in the five-and-ten and supported you and the kids it would be O.K."

Uh, Uh man—never cop out. *Never ever ever.* Not if you love your wife, 'cause chicks don't know anything about guys at all. All they know is about Billy Graham—the fantasy, you know, about the kind of Norman Rockwell people that never did exist. No, guys can make it on the highway. But chicks, the climate has to be just right. So if your old lady walks in on you, deny it. Yeah. Flat out. Just keep on denying—

HUSBAND: I'm tellin' ya, this chick came downstairs with a sign around her neck, LAY ON TOP OF ME OR I'LL DIE. I didn't know what I was gonna do.

WIFE: Will you get outta here, you dirty liar—and take that tramp with you.

HUSBAND: I'm lyin'? Ask Mrs. Slobowski to come down here! This chick came downstairs with this sign around her neck, LAY ON TOP OF ME I'M A DIABETIC, OR I'LL DROP DEAD. Now what was I gonna do, now?

WIFE: Well—O.K., just this once. But next time, keep the door locked and don't let those tramps in here anymore.

See, they'll believe you. Why? 'Cause they wanna. They wanna believe you.

Like Honey, who finally got out of the hospital and knew that Lenny had made it with the nurse's aide. But what was she gonna do? Kick him out? She loved the bastard, and that's the way he was.

CHAPTER 17

"YEAH. I WAS IN SHOCK FOR—THREE WEEKS, I THINK. I had these cuts all over my arms. My legs—a big gash right through, you know, my bladder. It was really bad. Yeah—it was very dramatic.

"But you know, they have these miracle drugs and all. The thread that melts right into you. I had physiotherapists and everything. It was a couple of months I was in there."

Yes, Honey made it.

Sure, she had to use a wheelchair for a while. Crutches. But only a while. That too passed, and the most miraculous thing of all was that her face, beaten up so badly it looked ready for meatloaf—her face was like they say, good as new.

Unspoiled—the *goyisha punim* Lenny was so crazy about.

They bought a new secondhand, slightly used 1951

fishtail Caddy Limousine with the seven thousand insurance smackers coming to them.

"A few more accidents like that, baby, and we're set for life," he tells her, and they're ready for the trip from the hospital parking lot to "The big Used-Car-Lot-In-the-Sky."

"California? Are we really going to California, Lenny?"

Well how else are they going to crack New York. Of course they're going to California.

Lenny still hadn't made it big. They still got showed the side door. The one saved for the help. But it's also the best part of their marriage. All across the country he does bits for her in the car. She cracks up. They're really happy.

They stop in dives along the route, he's schooling her how to make it under the spot without having to strip. If singing's not enough, he'll throw in a few jokes, how to play with the audience, how to just be up there and feel safe.

They're having a good time, Honey and Lenny. Life's being pretty good to them.

And there's something so American about the two of them. With all the put-it-down, let-nothing-go-by-the-boards *shticks* of his he succumbs himself, they both do, to the most American foible of them all.

From one town to the other, neither of them can stop touching the shiny fins on their new car. They're wild about it, keep running their hands down the uptown feel of the upholstery.

"Oh God, baby, it's the most." She rubs off a spot on the seat with a little spit and her little finger. For two hundred miles that's all he can talk about.

"I wanna tell ya little lady," he spritzes, "this here is the same car Ike and Dick drive in," and he slaps the dash, gunning it past seventy. "You take it from Fat Boy. Almost new—used only one time in a suicide pact, so maybe there's a li'l lipstick around the exhaust pipe—"

"Oh that's nothin', Fats, I can get that off with a little *Babo*." She's learning, Honey is. Pretty soon she'll be able to keep up her end of the punch line with the best of them.

"Thass right, Young Lady. A li'l *Babo* gonna fix this little creampuff up 112%."

"I'll take it."

"Smartest thing you ever did in your life."

"So, where we goin', Fat Boy?"

"Well there, young lady, first I'm takin' you to the motel, where I'm gonna give it to you the same way I been givin' it to the public for twenty-five years—and in the same location, too."

"You promise?" she giggles, reaches over and drops her tongue down his ear.

Except the good times never seem to have much staying power.

They gotta couple of gigs. They moved on. They gotta couple more gigs. But mostly if they wanted them at all the clubs only wanted Lenny. So pretty soon it was one of those dollar-a-night dives with signs from the war still sitting in the window: SERVICEMEN WELCOME. Honey was crapped out on the chenille spread upstairs. Lenny was booked into some nowhere joint giving them a few of the same jokes he'd given them the night before somewhere else—Illinois, Ohio. One on-the-way hole or another.

Suddenly Honey woke. It was about three and Lenny was back.

"Hi, baby," she said and then saw that he wasn't alone. He had some cat in a zoot suit in the head with him. A zoot suit with white suspenders and a black and white polka dot shirt. They're deep into something that's going on in there and without knowing what, she knows.

Last week, somewhere else, Lenny'd found some dude who'd sold them enough grass to stay out-of-it all the way to the Mississippi. But this guy had the real McCoy.

He had it and he didn't mind sharing.

First this guy, Lenny's silent partner, he took out a small packet of white powder and spilled it into the palm of his hand. Then he gave Lenny a straw.

She could feel Lenny's eagerness. He snorted so hard he almost got a nosebleed.

"Easy, man, easy," the guy said and Honey smiled. "Like this, baby—" and he gave them a demo. In two beats, Lenny was sniffing. She watched him and could see it hit.

Almost right away he got this fantastic look in his eye and about dragged her off the toilet seat so she could get a sniff herself.

"Jesus, try it baby. It's boss like you never dreamed."

So sure she tried it.

Boss? It was wild. Made peyote a downer. It was fantastic, made you feel like tickling each other to death. Made you wigged up, zonked out and finger-snapping at the same time. Made you ready to get out there and miss up on nothing.

For an hour. For an hour-and-a-half maybe, but by that time they still had sixteen hours till Lenny had to show up for work again. They were ready for the Howitzer. And besides, this cat was just the one to fix them up.

Back to the head.

Before he even sat down, Lenny had his sleeve up. The guy reached into a woman's make-up kit he kept in the lining of his raincoat and came up with all the fixings. Needles and syringes, tablets, bottles, soap, cotton batting, a tube to wrap around your arm. He had it all baby. All.

First he dumped another packet of powder into a teaspoon with a bent handle. Then he helped Lenny wrap the tubing around his arm while he lit a match and melted down the horse.

The veins in Lenny's, arm turned purple. He kept making a fist and unmaking it. The three of them stared down at the arm and then at the syringe and how this strange bird with his almost ballet-like motions sucked up the melted white powder from the spoon into the glass and then, finding an easy spot to hit, dug the needle into Lenny's arm and let go.

For a second nobody said anything. Honey was watching Lenny's eyes as if seeing a dying man's last thoughts—and then suddenly the eyes sank back into his head. All she could see was white. He sucked a long swallow of air through his nostrils and let out a long throbbing moan. It was her moan. The one that rose up out of her belly when he had it in her. When they'd just climbed as far as they could go and were going over the top.

"Better, baby," he screamed, "better"—and she couldn't stand it. By the time the guy had loosened the belt from Lenny's elbow and pulled out the syringe she had knotted the belt from her robe around hers and was jabbing it in the guy's face.

"Me too," she said fixing the two of them with naked hunger. "Comeon, you guys, hurry up and cook up another batch—I'm ready, I'm really ready."

CHAPTER 18

A KIND OF CHEVY MEDICINE SHOW. THEY WORKED A town, they moved on. They got high, they worked another town, they kept on going. In between Honey got pregnant.

"If there was any other way, wouldn't I do it? Comeon, baby, don't pull that anything-you-say shit— say something forcrissakes."

"I love you, Lenny."

"You don't think I love you? I wouldn't lie down on 66, my arms in a cross for you? Honey, don't—it's not fair—O.K., forget it. I won't say anything. You make the decision. Whatever you say. Comeon—I mean it."

"I dunno, Len, I could—"

"What?"

"You know, I—"

"Spell it out, baby, spell it out."

"They know I'm knocked up Lenny, I told you they know. And it's O.K. Honey I could make a bundle. Some guys love that."

"You're kidding me. You think I'm gonna let my wife—*on* the ramp out to there? *That's* the bottom baby, the bottom. Not *my* wife. If we never have a kid I'm not letting you parade your belly down to a G-string. So forget it. Besides I told you, knocked up or not knocked up, we'll make it without you stripping."

"But Lenny."

"Honey there's no buts. What? You think I don't want a kid? Wouldn't I cut off my nuts to have a kid? But not now, baby—not now."

"Lenny I'm six months gone."

"I told you—quit worrying. This guy is great. Call Lil. She's used him four times. Call her. You got nothing to worry about. And anyway, you know—I don't think I could love a kid as much as I do you. I couldn't love anybody like you, baby. With you, lovin's the only thing. It's like eatin' icecream, baby. Pistachio smothered in pink nipples."

So Honey got unpregnant.

And it wasn't so bad. Hadn't she gone from Hot Honey Harlow to Honey Michelle, the class singer? Besides Lenny said they'd have a kid. Only later, that's all. So O.K., she could wait.

And meantime they made a lotta stops. Sometimes they got into boosting. For kicks, that's all. No heavy for-real numbers or anything.

Lenny had a new connection. Boss horse, a dime toll and into the wind in three-quarter time—out of the club into the caddy and off. Sometimes they were popping uppers, to keep them through the boost.

Into a store, any store, splitting up and snaking in and out so smooth who could tell anything.

Caviar under a pound and a half of potatoes.

Sirloins under the armpit.

Zeniths between the thighs.

Kid stuff—but something to pass the time. In a dump like Orient, you had to have some kind of glue between highs.

"See baby," Lenny said, squeezing Honey's almost-good-as-new waistline.

"Didn't I tell you it'd be a ball?"

On their way from Death Valley to the West Coast Apple, a straight nonstopper. And then finally, finally, finally—

Gossip-column city: The strip, *The Derby, Chasen's*. They made it—driving around and around like two kids with a *Flexible Flyer* and an all-day sucker. Up the strip and down La Cienega. A quick turn over to Rodeo Drive and a long sideways gawk at the little old lady with the blue hair and the yellow Continental.

Like two tourists from Weehawken, they followed the bus to Bel Aire, which didn't look anything different than Roland Park in Baltimore. The same lawns, the same little *nigger* boys throwing rings sitting on them.

And they followed the bus out again. Names out of *Screen Romances: Romanoff's, Ciro's, Culver City*. Man, by the time they crapped out on the beach off East Wind Drive in Venice, they didn't need a high to feel great.

But they took one anyway, just a drop—for the hell of it.

"Before we're done with this town, sweetmeat, we'll have your jugs in cement in front of *Grauman's Chinese*. And no one will be allowed to walk on them," he said just before his nod turned into sleep.

"Sure, baby," she sobbed, all wrapped up in his arms. "Sure they will." And when Lenny asked her what was the matter, why was she crying, all she could figure out to say was:

"I'm so happy, that's all, baby. I don't know—I'm just so fucking happy—"

CHAPTER 19

"SO YOU LIKED CALIFORNIA?" THE INTERVIEWER ASKED her.

"Yeah, well it was really great. Wanna see a picture? I got a picture around here somewhere. A real little house and all—I mean we didn't go to L.A. to hang out on the beach. So we really did it, got ourselves pots and pans. You know, stuff like that. Dishes and all—housekeeping . . . it was, well I liked it. For a while it was, you know—terrific."

She smiled. Her funny little lap dog jumped up on the cot and licked her neck.

She looked so sad.

The tape recorder kept right on winding.

So they got a house.

A picket fence, a nest of porcelain and a couple of forks boosted from Schwabs. A real home. Squeezing, holding—and only sometimes with the drugs. Not into a regular habit or anything, just, like, for fun. For something to do when everybody got together.

Lying around.

Gorging on peanut butter and Ritz.

Yoohoos.

A little pistachio icecream—Jesus, but Lenny never could get enough pistachio and thinking about making it. Lying around in the dark with their feet up on each other, they'd listen to the Bird. Closing their eyes and beating time to *Ko Ko,* grooving on Miles, turning night into night, all the windows curtained, all the light bulbs unscrewed. When they weren't otherwise running around selling their act. The unbeatable duo: songsters, dancers, impressions—you name it mister, they could do anything and would. Except nobody was buying. Another song and dance team with top hats, homemade canes and a pretty face who couldn't do much. Who needed it?

So they dipped into savings. And they cut a couple of corners.

When they wanted to fix they'd cut out the peanut butter.

They made sacrifices.

And after a while they made a couple of other adjustments.

More and more they'd be in rooms that were really crowded. They'd pushed the studio couch against the wall and about eighty-three types would be on it. Long skinny babes in shrouds stitched together from old bedspreads, big fat babes with their boobs on their belly buttons, tiny little babes with those little lost faces, peeking out of uncombed hair, the scent of yesterday's candybar on their teeth. And the hipsters. With the white ducks and the dark shades. With the hair on their chests and the hair in their eyes. And the pot smoke you could trip on. And the "Yeah baby," and "Like, sure," and "Like, when," and "Like whatever you say, man."

And a couple, dry-humping on the floor next to the pick—

And three or four guess-what's groping around behind the couch in a stew.

And Lenny off in a corner with his finger up somebody else's broad.

And Honey off somewhere else underneath some
cat with an Apache headband.

"Groovy, baby—like man, the place is really wigging
out."

And a whole lot of blue and yellow capsules. And
red and green. And the little blue ones and the big
whites. And "who's got the meth?" and "when's he
coming?" and—

"Well, you know—you do things with dope that it
wouldn't ordinarily come into your mind to do."

Honey looked through this interviewer and his tape
recorder and saw again the little bedroom in the little
house, after everybody's gone. After she and Lenny
were all alone, except that by then everything was already different.

"Why not?"

"You know why not. I just don't want to, that's all."

"What are you scared of—comeon, it'll be nice."

"Why do you keep pushing this Lenny? You keep
pushing—"

At home and at work where Honey was back stripping—because they hadda eat, didn't they?—Lenny
pushed.

"I don't know. A little excitement—it'll be good for
both of us."

"Good?"

Honey sits before the mirror getting ready. Bingo
French, with tits out of a doctor's office, parades
around behind them, bending over, fixing her garters,
sticking her can in Lenny's face.

"I just don't think we can handle it," Honey says.

"Comeon, Lenny, why can't we just have it the way we used to."

"What's this Comeon Lenny shit. You know I love you. Don't you know I love you?"

"O.K., so I know it."

"Then we can handle it. We can handle anything."

Only you can see from Honey's eyes, she don't wanna. She don't think so and why can't he leave it alone, Lenny. Leave it alone.

And worse later—later when the two of them take the elevator to this chick's room. Where she's waiting with her little tits hanging there waiting for Honey's mouth. Waiting while Lenny watches. Waiting.

When Honey has to accept that the simple time is finished, letting the girl come to her, looking over the girl's shoulders to the insistent Lenny who insists. When Honey has to let up and let it happen. Let herself go. Go with it.

With her smell of squirrel and mouldy leaves on Honey's body.

With her fingers over Honey's long hair as red as tonsils. "Gowan," Lenny's eyes command her. "Gowan, you bitch, you know you love it."

And sure she loves it, the soft touch of this soft woman. The knowing fingers of someone who's been in the same places herself. Who lives in the same life. Who makes Honey come so easy and so nice that Lenny loathes her.

O.K., she loves it, but why? Lenny?

Lenny I love *you*, why can't you let love-enough alone.

Coming and crying at the same time, Why Lenny? I don't want to feel so good not under your hands. Don't make me love this Lenny. Stand between me and me. Know what I need and give it to me.

And later—after—when they were home again.

CHAPTER 20

"SONAVABITCH!"

The sound of the middle-size pot, banging against the stove. Chipping bits of porcelain. Cracking through to the black.

"You can't let life alone. You can't."

"Quit the hysterics."

Throwing it at him. Missing and then crashing through the French doors into the bed.

In tears. In more tears.

"You're a spoiler, you bastard. The minute you have something good you've gotta slit its throat."

"Who's the spoiler and quit throwing that crap or I'll break your arm," he screamed. "I didn't see you running for the fuzz, baby. And I didn't see anybody raping anybody either."

"You creep. Oh, you lousy creep."

"Who's calling who what?"

"You made me, you bastard—you know GD-well you made me."

"Made you? Oh comeon, Honey-love. Where's the

bruises on that snow-white body of yours?"

"You and your lousy freak scenes."

"Yeah, well who's the freak?"

Too much. She bangs her head down on the wall. She's throbbing with tears.

"Damn you, Lenny. Oh God—damn you!" as he goes right on dressing. After all he's finally got a gig. A solo.

"I knew it. I knew this would happen, Lenny—I knew it."

Her voice was suddenly as quiet as a lily.

"I told you."

"Yeah, you told me. But you forgot to mention how much you were gonna dig it."

"Oh God, Lenny—"

She was shaking her head back and forth and lying on the floor like spilled milk.

"Oh God, Lenny, you're crazy. What do you want from me, baby? All you have to do is tell me—what the hell is it you want from me?"

"Want? What makes you think I want anything. Well ah—I gotta be going, got to run through that new business tonight. You know the one—about the dykes? What's the look for, I like dykes. Me and Will Rogers." He walked over to the table and getting up on a chair next to it, took a position like the Statue of Liberty.

" 'I never met a dyke I didn't like.' You dig it? It's a big laugh see, and then I say how a lotta comics'll do these endless fag jokes but how everybody leaves the dykes alone and how the reason for it is—" And he gets down off the chair and gives Honey a blister with his eyes.

"See the reason is dykes'll really kick the shit outa ya, and—oh yeah. It's hard to spot them a lot too 'cause ah—'cause sometimes we're married to them."

"You BASTARD—you fucking lousy Bastard!"

"And I made it with that chick in the hospital. You didn't know that did you?"

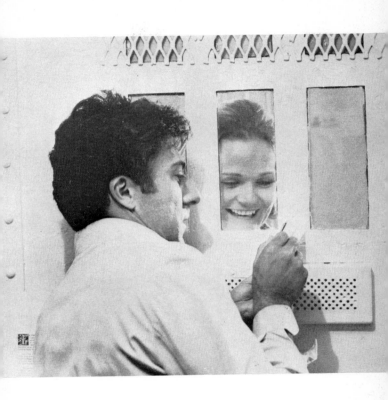

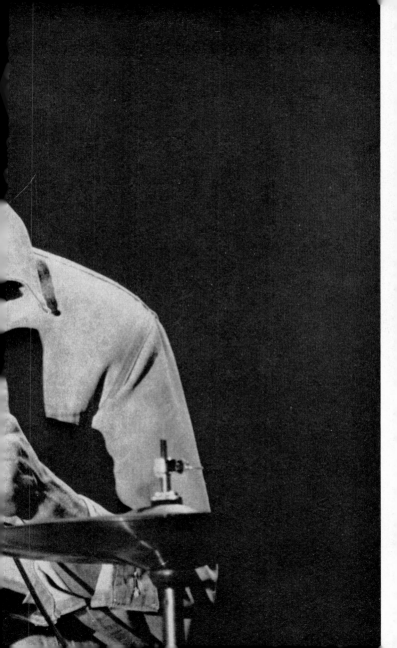

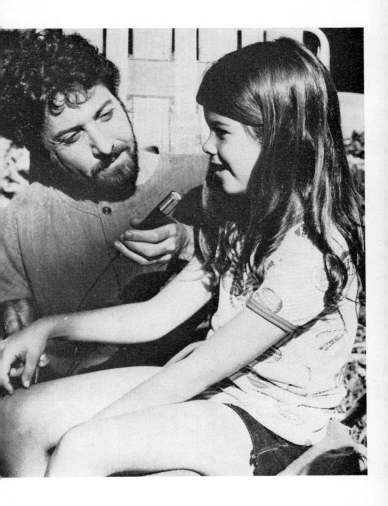

"I knew it."

"And so fucking many other chicks your head'd spin, baby—so why don't we even things up. I told you my score. Now it's your turn."

"Oh Lenny, I told you—"

"No gowan baby. I can take it."

"Lenny I don't wanna play this game. Honey, what's happening to us, why are we making all these—these weird scenes. Lenny—"

"Comeon Honey, I'm broad-minded. Don't you want to tell me about what's-her-face? The one with the tattoo on her thigh and the bar bells—and those cute little combat boots—"

"Please, I love you, I love you. You should tell me to stop. Stop me Lenny—Lenny"—and she's wrapped around his leg like a heap of dirty sheets.

"You gotta do it by yourself."

"Help me, Lenny. Please—help me."

"Oh shit, why should you—just because I say so? You know you dig it—and what's wrong with it? Why should you stop?"

He pulls her arms from around him and begins to go for the door.

"Oh baby," she moans, in the saddest voice. A voice that would melt Lot's wife. "Why do you always have to be so fucking hip?"

And it gets to him. He stops by the door, turns around and comes back to her, sinking down on his knees and taking her in his arms.

"We're such bastards, you and I," he moans, and then pulls her into his kiss with a kind of morbid desperation.

"But I love you. Jesus H. Christ how I love you . . ."

And as he took off whatever it was she had on, and as they made the best love they'd made in a long time, Honey kept whispering, "I want a baby, Lenny. I've always wanted a baby. Now, baby—make me a baby now."

6

CHAPTER 21

"SO WE BOTH CLEANED UP FOR A WHILE, AND KITTY was born. It was 1956. We were like a real family for a while. Yeah—then Lenny started MCing in strip joints—real dives—so we didn't see each other very much and—I don't know."

The interviewer watched her. He'd talked to how many people in that business? But something about Honey's hopeless gestures touched him. As she caressed her silly little dog. As she fumbled stupidly in the box, for this or that worn-out picture of this or that worn-out memory. He was watching a woman relive the story of a life she never had a real bead on. A life that ran away with her.

"Well, some things just don't work out, you know? And you never seem to know why—"

She stopped talking and looked up at him. As if maybe he knew why. As if somewhere, at some particular moment, she was going to find out.

CHAPTER 22

SO, AS THEY SAY IN THE STORY BOOKS, THE STORK waited nine months and then brought them a beautiful little girl, whom they called Kitty.

And Kitty they really dug. As a matter of record, Kitty was such a high, that for a while Lenny and Honey started playing house just like their next door Joneses.

Honey changed Kitty's diapers and Lenny went to work in a strip joint. Then Lenny changed Kitty's diapers just 'cause he dug her so much. And the three of them ate out a lot. At *Hung Ho*'s, or *Sing Hi*'s, or one Chinese restaurant or another. And sometimes they brought home pizza. Or whatever else they could get to go. Just like a real family.

But then little things started to go wrong. Like for instance Lenny's job. Being an MC at a bummer strip joint wasn't a big turn-on for a guy who thought of himself as more than a piece of scotch tape between four tits. Because what else did he do? He'd be beating his chops to the elbow for them but those slobs weren't dropping their sheckels to hear some stud, they were there for the meat-market, man, so all he was supposed to do was innurduse the sides of beef, fellah—innurduse the protein.

And on top of it he wasn't home a hell of a lot. The hours, the guys he ran around with. Musicians, cats—hell, they didn't have no Kittys at home. With them it was "go baby go." So sometimes Lenny kinda went with it. That and his general depression about his work and everything. It was really getting to him.

And then Honey started hanging out too. I mean, she wasn't working, she was young, she was still a looker—

"What am I supposed to do, Lenny, sit around here getting gray while you're out there slinging the *shticks?*"

"What slinging? I'm working, baby, working. Ever heard of it?"

"Lenny even a sewer shuts down once in a while."

"That's a reason I should come home and find the kid screaming blue in the face and nobody's home. Nobody? Fahcrissakes, you bitch, she coulda choked to death for all you care."

"Fuck you, Lenny. Just plain and simple fuck you."

Except they didn't a whole lot in those days. They just kind of drifted: Lenny tighter with the boys in the band, Honey with whatever floated by.

The long turquoise convertible screeched to a stop in front of the *Tiki Kai,* leaving two long tire burns up Ensenada. The groovy redhead with her neckline down to her belly button leaned over so that nobody passing by could miss what was what. Then she laughed and practically jammed them into the cat's mouth.

"They think they own the streets, those people," somebody said.

And hated it because the cat was black.

"Black? That bastard's not black. He is so black you'll find smudge marks on that bitch's boobs—that's how black that woolly head is."

Except it's not woolly. It's conked and greased and down to a roller coaster wave. And she's got on shades and nothing much else. And it's "disgraceful—downright disgraceful the way they let these people drag the country downhill in a bushel basket."

Inside the restaurant Lenny's got the baby propped up in one of those plastic chairs. He is doing a looking-at-his-watch, looking-out-the-window, tapping-his-fingers number. He is pissed. I mean, here he is being the model father. He's minding the store, it's time to go to work and where the fuck is she?

"That bitch, knocking off every cock that winks at her."

"No, dum dum," he suddenly smiles at the baby. She's taken a sparerib and is sticking it into her ear. Her little dress is covered with rice—and her hair, and her eyes and everything else. Rice. Chop suey. It's everywhere. Lenny turns his attention in her direction and suddenly warms. He takes the rib out of her ear and gently gets it into the right opening.

"Good?" he asks her, and she kicks her little feet and almost burns them on the teapot. Daddy moves the teapot.

"Mmmmm good."

He takes her foot and mimics her with the rib. He sucks on her toes. He licks her calf. And then the waiter walks by.

"Hey, man. What time is it?"

"Sic-thirty."

Sic thirty—shit—where the hell is she? They were supposed to have dinner at a quarter of. Forcrissakes he s got an early call. What's the matter with that bitch?

Nothing. That bitch has just stuck her tongue into the stud's ear and then finished up the job with a face

wash. And she's still laughing. Louder even as he lets
her out of the car and pulls away leaving her a little
high, a lot used and not quite together.

"Don't be mad, Daddy," she says as she slides into
the booth. And now come the excuses. But it doesn't
matter. One look at her eyes and it doesn't matter
what she comes up with. It isn't exactly that Lenny
hasn't been there. When it comes to horse—what can
she say?

"—a cab . . ."

She couldn't get a cab. She called three places. They
said they'd send one. You know how they are these
days. Unreliable, he hears, but from unreliable—he
wrote the book. And he sits there and watches her
nodding off, giggling as if listening to an old joke.
And then she nods off again, she's scratching her face,
and she passes him the saddest smile he's ever seen.

He gives the baby a spoonful of fried rice.

"I finally got one, Daddy. Here I am," she says.

"Sure," he answers her. "Sure."

CHAPTER 23

LENNY'S GOT PROBLEMS. HONEY'S GOT PROBLEMS. Kitty's got a lotta problems.

Anyway Lenny's gotta go to work. He's gotta be funny. Later he can get to a phone. Call the sitter. Find out, did she eat? How's her diarrhea? What about the diaper rash?

He knows Honey's not home. Honey knows the same about him. They're living together, but they're not living together and both hope that somewhere Kitty's too little to know any different.

The first stripper moves out. Lenny gets her her hand, and then moves into his Lawrence Welk number. Things are changing out there in the audience. Sure mostly the guys still wanna check out only the girls—but here and there, there and here, he's getting a response. He gets the idea somebody besides the guys in the band know there's somebody up there—

WELK: Wunnaful, wunnaful, wunnaful . . . Awright, send in da new boy. Hello, Sonny, how are you?

And ah, we got a nize band here, just like one big happy family—everybody ball everybody else's ol' lady. And ah, da agent send you over and told me you be perfect boy for my band—you're deaf. Awright, we gonna go right on da road, so—wotsa matter wit you, Sonny, how come you don't talk to me?

JUNKIE: Well, you know, like ah—a lotta cats put you down, Mr. Wack, but ah—no matter what they say, ah—you're the best banjo player, and ah —whatever your axe is, man—I know you swing . . . and like, I knew Bird very well, man—I got Bird's axe. I knew all them people. I knew Miles, man—I knew Basie 'fore he could count, ha ha ha—ain't I wild? O.K., so like, what d'you say, sweetie, like ah—we make the scene, baby, huh— you dig?

WELK: What da hell are you talkin' about?

JUNKIE: Hey, ah—you pretty wild, Polack, ha ha ha.

WELK: Hey, what d'you keep scratching your face for?

JUNKIE: I'm allergic, man, I mean—I'm a nervous cat, and ah—I don't wanna bug ya, man, but ah— you think I could get a little bread up front?

WELK: You hungry? You wanna sandwich?

JUNKIE: No, ah—(laughs) I want some money—ah, see, wait 'til you get to know me, man. I'm really a goodnatured slob, and ah—I need some money to, ah—to take my aunt to the hospital, ah—look at her, man, she's out in the car throwing up— out there, man. So, ah—let's do the thing, man. What d'ya say, baby, let's make it—

WELK: Awright, I'm going to sign you 'cause I'm a good judge of character. You're an honest boy—I can tell by your eyes, they's so small. And I like the way you dress—dat's Ivy League, with the belt on the arm—

JUNKIE: Yeah, well ah—I hate to cop out on myself,

man, but ah—I better tell ya in front, I got a monkey on my back.

WELK: Oh, dat's awright, we like animals on da band. Rocky's got a duck—they'll play together.

And sure, he was beginning to bring them in. He hit it and then hit it again. The junkie who was always scratching. Everybody who knew the Bird. (Was there one bastard who even played *Fur Elise* on the out-of-tune upright who didn't used to hang out with Charlie? At least have one ride in a cable car with him?)

That kind of thing. Lenny could look right through them—right down to everybody's skeleton.

Life rolls on. One day. Another. Some more pizza. Tacos on the half shell. And then back to their chop suey emporium. After Lenny maybe has himself a fix. Nothing atomic. Maybe not even with a needle. Just a little something to get him through till tomorrow.

In the same booth. Eating the same *moo goo gai* mush.

"Where's the Missus?" the waiter wants to know. "She's the prettiest girl I ever see. Is Missus sick? You take these fortune cookies and tell her I say hello to her. She's a wonderful wife, Missus. You tell her I say hello."

"We're divorced," is how Lenny tells it, to which inscrutable says without a beat, "You better off."

End of marriage.

End of bit.

CHAPTER 24

HONEY'S VOICE HAD SHIFTED THREE OCTAVES. SHRILL.
Confused.

"I don't know why. He just—he took her from me.
We were in the islands, I had some trouble—"

Her voice begins to head back down to middle C.
The flash of anger seeps out the bottom. Her hands
unclench and lie very quietly in her lap.

"He knew I—they wouldn't let me. He—"

The interviewer could hardly hear her.

"He and Kitty—:"

"Ahh Honey, the tape just ran out. I didn't get all
of that. Would you—I mean give me a minute and
then—"

"Hey, forget it. I know why. We both knew I
couldn't look after her."

Hawaii had been the last for them. Everything run
down to the ground and then under. No connections

90

for the hard stuff. Having to live it out up front, just the raw dregs—no icing. Honey even more desperate than Lenny, running around like a typhoon just to cop a little weed—anything to deal with the motherhood, with the stone weight of what was left of their marriage. And then her clincher—the man puts a pot collar to her.

For six lousy joints.

And then hassles her she should finger the connection: "It'll go easier on you, lady, what's more important, a couple of years in the hole or some suede-suited stud out there, living off your hump?"

Honey's worst moment. Knowing she was held fast and there goes Lenny with Kitty—further and further out of earshot, out of touch. Left only the wrankling fears, onaccounta . . . "Who'd pull a sneak stunt like that?" she wanted to know. "Who could hate a person so much?" After all hadn't she been cleaner than Rinso White for three weeks before she'd tripped over those six incriminating reefers? How come they knew, just like that, Little Boy Blue with his heavy hand?

While Lenny was out hustling bail. While he assured her,

"Gowan, nothing's going to happen to a mother with a little baby and a home that depended on her not going to the lock-up."

"I'd kill myself," he assured her.

For a while he held her in his arms again as if her body grew out of his.

"If you ever went away from me, Honey, I swear to God, I'd kill myself."

He held her and absented himself with the same fell swoop. Because it was all inevitable. Their things were long broken down before Honey's bust. Broken and finished—so that one day Honey turned around and Lenny and the baby were gone. For good and all, and she couldn't even call,

"Lenny—I love you Lenny—"

She couldn't because her bail wouldn't let her leave

Hawaii and because Lenny, when he got back to L.A., had his phone disconnected.

"Don't leave me, Lenny," Honey called as the legal procedure proceeded.

"Don't leave me"—except the operator answered only,

"I Yam Sorry—" with that dial-a-blank-wall voice, of theirs. "The number you have dialed is not in service at this time."

And after that, the time when his phone was working overtime. When, if it wasn't Honey, desperate from Hawaii, allavasudden he'd inherited a Jewish mother.

"So, Lenny?"

"What is it, Ma?"

"So how come you're playing L.A., Lenny? I thought you were—"

"I was."

"Not we? Lenny? Where's—"

No answer.

"Oh . . . So Lenny? How's the baby?"

"She's O.K. Ma."

"You know Lenny?"

"What?"

"Did I tell you, I'm thinking of moving to California, Lenny?"

Sally Marr turning grandma. First of all, getting a tint. Sally Marr wasn't going to show up looking like the kind of grandmother even the wolf wouldn't swallow. A tint, a couple of beaded crepes. A manicure. Yeah, Lenny needed her, but she wasn't going to California like some *yenta* yokel.

Not that Mema approved: "What's the matter with you, Sally? You're going to give up your life?"

"What life? That's my life now, Mema, I have it coming to me. A grandchild to play paddycake with. Besides I'll be near Lenny. It's not the worst thing in the world, Mema, and who or what's stopping me?

This nothing I have here is such a deal?"

"You know I never thought I'll live to see the day you'll be a Jewish mother, Sally. I'm telling you, I'm very much surprised. And what about Lenny? You told him?"

"Told him? Are you kidding with Lenny, Mema, when he heard I was coming, he was so happy, I thought he'd cry."

"He needs me Mema. For the first time my Lenny needs ME."

Or at least a complimentary charge plate with AT&T. Every day, every minute more phone calls. Expensive phone calls. From Honolulu to L.A. From L.A. to Honolulu.

"I have a collect call for a Mr. Lenny Bruce from Mrs. Lenny Bruce in Honolulu. Will you accept the charges?"

"Yeah—yeah." After the hesitation. After the steel hard look in his eye, Kitty in the other room, Sally on her way.

"Sure—sure." What was he going to do with that need of her's—strung out, up tight, on one thing or another. Always with the chocolate coating her teeth. The coke rotting her gums. He has a choice? He cannot accept the charges?

"Hello Lenny? Lenny, this is Honey. Hello Lenny?"

And who was he kidding? How many times did *he* cradle the receiver in the crook of his neck so he could fix and talk at the same time? How many times? leaning back and letting the shit hit as she reached out for his jugular through the wires—this beat-up broad of his, DTing out there in her Honolulu hell. Not a question of who's walking the straight and narrower. A question of what, Honey? In your flowered rag, up your creek, down to the bitter grounds.

And finally her voice.

"What's shakin' baby?"

"Honey, you called me—"

Up to his eye teeth in kid piss.

"Lenny, do you love me?"

"Sure, I love you, but you're killing me with phone bills. It's eight times this week, already, Honey. It ends up I'm breaking my balls just to keep AT&T on the big board."

And called again when he just walked in the door. When he's done three shows, been up and down on four different pills and looked forward to one good night's sleep the way a kid wants Christmas.

The phone ringing before he's through the door. The phone ringing and the phone ringing.

"Will you accept the charges? Mr. Bruce?"

"Mr. Bruce, will you accept the charges?"

"Just a minute, Operator," he says so he can kick off his shoes and lie down in the dark so not to wake up the kid. The kid he was fighting in the courts to get custody of. The kid everytime he looked at he got a stab. The same *goyisha punim* as that desperate one out there on the other end of the line around her throat.

Yeah, he was ready to accept the charges. "Yeah, Honey? So how're you doing?" Only *don't* tell him. To accept the charges was as far as he could handle. He was stretched thin, Honey—thin.

"What are you doin'? Lenny? Do you miss me?"

"Sure I miss you. I told you I miss you. Honey, I'll write you a letter."

"No, don't hang up Lenny. Hey Lenny are you working?"

"Oh comeon Honey, I told you three days ago— I'm working Duffy's."

"Oh yeah, I forgot. Terrific. Gee that's—Lenny?"

"What?"

"I got some good news. I met this agent see, and he thinks he can book me, you know—conventions and stuff—"

"Yeah, I know. You told me."

"I did? Oh. Well, anyway, he says it's almost definite. I'd be great Lenny, I'd be making some bread.

Anyway, he said he'd call this weekend—Lenny?"

"Yeah, it's terrific. It's really terrific."

"Yeah, but the really good news is this. See, my lawyer says maybe I won't have to go to jail. He says we can appeal, only—"

"Only what?"

"—well, see—well it's gonna take more money. And, look I hate to bother you again, only—"

"How much is it gonna be this time?"

"A coupla hundred?"

"Yeah—well look, I'll do what I can."

He's shaking his head and clenching his teeth. It's the same phone call. He could make a record and play his end back next time. Next time and next time and the time after that.

"I'll pay you back this time. You know, I'll be working—I mean this guy he said he'd call this weekend, and—"

She's crying out there and he doesn't know who he hates more, her or himself.

"I miss you, Daddy."

She's killing him.

"How's Kitty?"

"Swell."

"You change her a lot? You gotta change her a lot or she gets—she gets those rashes—"

"I gotta hang up now."

Hang, hang it up. "I gotta go Honey," let go a-my-balls. I'm dyin' baby. I can't take any—

"Lenny?"

"Yeah—I'm still here."

"Lenny, do you still love me?"

"Sure, yeah, I love you, Honey, I gotta hang up. I can't cut it with these phone bills. It never stops, baby. It's drowning me, it's—"

"Because I still love you, Lenny. So, you know—as soon as I'm straight—"

"Listen—I'll send what I can, O.K.?"

"O.K." Tiny-tot, baby, *nebbish*, voice drowning in

95

salt water slicing through his heart—his walls, his brain.

"Take care of yourself," which is a laugh if you come right down to it—or even close.

    . . . I tell ya . . . it's really hard when you break up with your old lady. At first you think, "O.K., that's groovy. Screw her—I'll really swing now. But the kind of chicks you meet when you're divorced are divorced chicks, and they all live with their mother who is also divorced.
Either that or they can never have you over to the house because they have a kid. Or if they do have you over they make you go in the bedroom and watch him sleep. He's sweating in those pajamas with the grape jelly on them—that really kills the whole fantasy.
Every divorced chick I know has that six-year-old kid—it's like a prop from Central Casting. Or, if they don't have a kid, they have a French poodle that has to be allowed in the bedroom.
GUY: Ah—excuse me, but, ah—what is the function of this dog?
CHICK: He's only a little dog. He won't bite you. He just wants to watch.
GUY: Wants to watch?! Get outta here, pervert!!! I'm not an exhibitionist.
LENNY: Sick, red eyes—tap dancing on the linoleum floor. (does the dog)
Dumb French poodles. No, it's—I tell ya—if you been married for five years, and it goes into the shithouse, then you're just gonna spend a lot of time throwing up, because nobody goes into a marriage with the idea of blowing it. And when it's over, about the only satisfaction you can have is to get custody of that kid—but custody is a lot of dues, Jim.
Custody means, "I love, I raise, I clean, I get up in the morning, I make the breakfast—" Oh yeah.

Custody.

It also means it's finished, Honey. It means the real world. It means Sally's coming to stay. It means kindergarten and bills and living in two worlds at the same time, out there and home. Hard, it means. Kitty is a person sleeping in a crib with sheets and rubber mats and disposable nipples on her bottles. Work. Debts. Grow up. Keep going.

You see the trouble is we live in a "Happy Ending" culture instead of a "what is" culture. But people don't stay—

No different than Leonard and Harriet on the little gold matchbook covers. It's true, as he tucks the small child into her nighttime dreamland. On stage or off—
People don't stay.

CHAPTER 25

"SO, YOU CAME TO L.A.?"

"Lock and stock. Came to L.A., took up grandmothering. It was great. I saw a lot of Lenny. Kitty and I got to, you know, really know one another. Best thing I ever did, coming to L.A. And exciting too. You know, Lenny was at Duffy's. Sure, it was only a strip joint but the *shtick* he used to do between strippers—"

"What kind of stick?"

"*Shtick*, darling—*shtick*. The girls, they'd finish their number, Lenny'd come out, get them a big hand and then he'd come on a while. He really began to open up at Duffy's. Yeah, I'd say that's where his style really began to change. He stopped doing that traditional stuff—you know, routines-off-the-rack—and he just, you know—he just started to improvise."

Sally Marr, Sally Marsalle, Boots Malloy. There she sat, the tape recorder recorded and the interviewer looked at her. She had the thick skin of a woman over the bloom. Her hair was out of a bottle. Her figure a lot thicker than it used to be, but she still had a lot going, Lenny's Jewish mother. She had a good substantial look in her eyes. A way of laying it all clean out, of moving in with the heavy artillery right from GO. Lenny's old lady was a regular guy. A person could do a lot worse.

She began to remember a lot about the toilet Lenny was working at the time—Duffy's, way out on the strip. Sure she remembered Duffy's, that was back when Lenny went from paying the rent to the big time.

Know what I just thought of?

(Lenny picks up a chair sitting over by the piano, and holds it up for the audience.)

Here's a wild thought: You know how many asses have been on this chair? Oh man, there have been a lot of asses on this chair. Now you and I have no way of knowing how many, but lions and tigers know. That's why when Frank Buck goes (he holds up the chair as if fending off 3 tons of killer cat), they go: Pwheeeew, vvvaggghauuuuh—

And not only the band cracks up. O.K., it's still a strip joint. Sally's going back a long time. Mostly they don't know from Lenny Bruce, these *shmucks*. They're here to see tits and ass. Goway with the chairs and the concepts, there. But there's a few out there besides the band. And the others are just around the corner. Sally's come into the picture just before it began to get a lot more colorful.

And now ladies and gentlemen—the moment you've been waiting for. We're going to bring you a lovely lovely lady. This girl has everything: beautiful skin, lovely teeth—and a slight case of the syph. So careful not to touch her. And here she is—Wanda and her bird!

See Wanda's bird?

See Lenny go backstage where he takes a little pill,

sits at the dressing table and gets a bit of about-time news from Artie.

"I'm telling you Lenny, they want you."

"Get outahere—they want me. They wanna use my balls for the pool table, they want me."

"I'm telling you, *shmuck*, it's finally happening."

"Forget it. I dig this toilet. Lissen, I can say anything I want. Anything that comes into my head. Nobody's listening anyway. You'll book me into some uptown joint and—"

"What if I could get you $750 a week."

"You're putting me on. What would they pay me $750 for?"

"To say anything that comes into your head—they really dug you."

"How d'you know?"

"They were here last week. I'm telling you, they think you're gonna become some kind of 'in' thing. Who knows—Lenny, let me call them."

"And no mother-in-law jokes?"

"Straight shit. Look man, try it. It's better off than cracking up three musicians for ninety bucks a week . . ."

"O.K. call them" he says and the next thing on his back is Sally.

"You're still gonna talk to me, bigshot?"

"What bigshot?"

"Are you kidding? Lissen, the way Artie tells it, another three weeks and Uncle Milty's gonna apply maybe you need a dresser."

"Very funny, Ma. Very funny."

"Who's funny, Lenny, I'm telling you. He says this new *shticklach* you're pulling, it's really gonna pay, Lenny."

"Yeah. Well so far my tax man ain't worried."

"So when am I gonna see you?"

"I told you, we'll call up Mrs.—"

"Well if you want my opinion I don't see what's the big deal."

"Look, Ma, I don't want her in the club, that's all. I just don't."

"What will she know, Lenny; she'll sleep—"

"I just don't like it, that's all."

"What's not to like? I'll give her her bottle. I'll wrap her up like an Indian. You said yourself she could sleep through a hurricane. I mean, what's the *shtuss*, Lenny, I'll take her for an hour. I'll see the show, I'll come back—what do we need to call a woman?"

"You know you drive me crazy. You hand me, 'Lenny you need me.' 'Lenny, what are you turning to outsiders?' O.K., so you come. And now that you're here, all you know is running."

"A lousy hour?"

"Never mind. Forget it. Do what you please."

"You know it's always the same thing with you. You have to have your own way. From the time you were—O.K. forget it—Lenny? Lissen, Artie told me about Honey."

"Yeah."

"What rotten luck. Who would think she could pull two years just for a couple of joints. Would you believe it? That bastard—when did it happen?"

"It happened. What's the difference when."

"Two years. It's a long time, two years at her age—especially for a woman."

"You know you're so full of shit. What do you mean, her age? Two years is a long time at any age."

"She was a nice girl, Honey. Real class. You know I—"

"Oh come off it. You couldn't wait to deep-six her. And she's not dead either forcrissakes. So O.K., she pulled a bum rap. But her life's not exactly over you know. It's not as if she got ten to twenty."

"But what I don't understand is how come they knew? It's funny, you know what I mean?"

"Lay off, Ma. I'm telling ya, lay the fuck off."

"What did I say?"

No answer. Pause. Look.

"So where'd they send her?"

"Terminal Island."

"Tsktsk . . ." then another. "So—so, Lenny?"

"Yeah?"

"I wanna ask you something but I'm afraid you'll get mad."

"I won't get mad."

"Promise?"

"Goddammit Sally, what the fuck is it?"

"Lenny, look, I'm your mother. O.K., so I never won any blue ribbons but don't tell me I don't want the best for you."

"Get to the point."

"The point? Well, Lenny, the point is—I looked in the medicine chest the other day. I cut my finger, I was looking for a bandaid—Lenny? What's all those bottles? I never saw so many bottles of pills in my life. What do you need them for, Lenny? Baby? What's going on with you? The next thing you know *you'll* pull in the narcs."

"What narcs? Can't you read? Can't you see they're prescription? Every GD bottle out there, prescribed by a doctor? What's this narcotics shit. I get this chest thing, I can't breathe—so I take a coupla pills. You know you're flippin' out Sally. In front of my eyes you're turning into Mema. Six more months and you'll be sprouting hair from your chin."

"It's no joke Lenny, the pill business. You listen to your mother, she knows what's best for you."

"Anything else?"

Wasn't it enough?

Yeah. It was enough.

His kid's mother was in jail. His kid, who could do a buck and wing but didn't know *Mary Had a Little Lamb* from *Wanda and her bird*. His kid's grandmother got heavier every minute.

So O.K.—he knew too many pills spoil the soup. But he also knew there's a point at which the gas tank is either half empty or full. Going back or heading for the hills, it's all the same headache. You pays your dues and you steps over the edge. Going anywhere but ahead was nowhere.

Who needed it?

CHAPTER 26

Anne's 440. 1958. HIGH-IQ FRISCO.

Wall-to-wall beatniks. Shades. Black turtlenecks. The hornrimmed bottle-bottom egghead specs and the "in" responses.

Truckloads of "you and me" looks. "Like Wow's" and "Like did I tell you?"

I mean just to look at him, this Arab-looking exotic in the beard. With the Nehru jacket. Here was one of their own, man. Somebody they could really get on with.

Eisenhower? Man, he's totally out of it. The students keep bugging him about the bomb, he doesn't even know where they keep the bomb. He knows where his old army jacket is, he remembers how to salute—and that's it. Actually though, it isn't a bomb, it's a button—a button on the fly of a Boy Scout somewhere, and some day the whole world is gonna go up because of some faggot Boy Scout Master.

Fast. You know. In and out with the voice. That New York street voice on the guy. They dig him. He swings.

But I dig what they do with homosexuals in this country. They put them in jail with a lot of men. Yeah—that's what I call good punishment.

Anne's 440 never had it so good.

CHAPTER 27

1959. LENNY SWINGS ON. THIS TIME THE CELLAR IS THE same except the audience has moved a notch. Up? Down? That's a matter of perspective. There are a lot more suits. A lot more striped ties and button-down collars. The moons on the fingernails are mani-cured. The women wear bottled scent. O.K., maybe he's not so avant -garde anymore, but he's making a lot more money.

He holds up a Sunday comic section and shows it to the audience. In the corner an engineer is record-ing the performance.

You know who I'd really love to get in front of the House Un-American Activities Committee?

He hasn't even gotten to the punch and they're laughing. It's '59. In the smart crowd just the initials HUAC bring a laugh. It's called how to keep from crying.

Daddy Warbucks.

(And then he comes on with his singsong Senator voice):

SENATOR: Now Daddy, will you tell this Committee what's really going on at your place with you and that little Orphan Annie and the weird little dog that keeps going "Arf"? Are you really her Daddy? Uh huh, that's what I thought. O.K., you've been having sex parties, isn't that it? Well tell me Warbucks, how come she has no eyes? Her eyes are always rolled back in her head. That's ecstasy, right?

"Oh Daddy—oh, Daddy, Daddy"—and the dog keeps going "arf." "Arf" means "next," right?

Yeah, right. Or at least close to it judging by the crush in the dressing room. The fans, the showbiz luminaries. Do we have to mention Sally? The ever-present Artie? And especially the girls. Who wanna grab. A touch of the funny fellow. Who wanna call him a comic genius and then go home and tell the girls in the office how they said it.

It's true what they said about Lenny becoming an "in" thing. If this was "in."

CHAPTER 28

IT'S GOTTEN TO BE 1960. LENNY'S WEARING DIFFERENT
clothes. The club has a different name. They charge
more for a screwdriver and it costs besides just to
walk through the door. But it doesn't seem to keep
people from queuing up to get in.

Are there any niggers here tonight? I—let's see:
there's two niggers, sitting next to two kikes, and
I see six polacks and—yeah, four micks. Lessee
four micks and three greaseballs—and there's two
more niggers—
(O.K. he builds it. He gets a little auctioneer patter
to it.)
There's two kikes and three niggers and one spic
(Adds a gambler) :
I pass with six niggers, eight micks and four wops.

At first the audience doesn't know how to take him.
And then they look around to see if anybody else
does. From anybody else they'd have hit out with the
ballbats a long time ago, these white, upper-brained,

better-educated liberals. How dare he, after they worked so long for so little—

You wanna know the point? I'll tell you the point.

There's an audible sigh through the cellar. See. They knew there was a point.

Suppression, man. Suppression of the word. That's what gives it its violence.

They sigh. All the reform democrats. They're vindicated.

Dig, if Kennedy would just go on TV and—
JFK: Ah (Big Boston tone) I'd uh like to introduce you to all the Niggahs in my cabinet.
LENNY: Sure. Yeah. If he yelled, "Nigger, niggerniggernigger" at every nigger. "Boogeyboogeyboogey," then maybe the word nigger would lose its clout. And nobody would ever be able to make some six-year-old black kid cry because somebody called him a nigger in school.

Wild applause, shrieks and foot-stomping—except Lenny's big number's to let the bastards figure it out for themselves. What was he, their nana?

Like the time some horse's ass reviewer said he understood "The middle-class dilemma."

"Whatever that means," he said to Artie. "Whatever the fuck that means."

Artie was on the telephone talking to a club owner. Artie's very cool to the mouthpiece, while his leg's hitting the underside of the table.

"I can give you a thousand a week," this joker's saying while Lenny listens in on the other phone, his hand cupped over the mouthpiece.

Lenny shakes his head, "forget it," to Artie, who tells the guy in his best manager's manner:

"Well, you see we were thinking in terms of—thirteen—"

Lenny's just shaking his head nonstop. He holds up five fingers.

"Well, what I meant was—uh, fifteen. Fifteen hundred minimum guaranteed against a percentage."

"What do you mean percentage?"

Lenny signals a big Two Oh.

"Twenty percent," Artie tells the guy, trying hard not to crack up. Twenty percent? He's figuring his ten percent of Lenny's twenty. With up-and-comers like his buddy here, a guy could get rich.

"Comeon, you gotta be kiddin'. Twenty percent. The guy's a fad—like hoola hoops. Twenty percent—"

Which pisses Lenny off. He moves the ante up to thirty.

"Did I say twenty? Well, the fact is, I meant to say thirty. That's what he wants. Thir—"

"Thirty percent? I can't live with that. I mean, comeon—that's so far out of line."

"Well, you know Lenny. He's—"

And Lenny makes the sign of the pencil sharpener against his temple.

"He's crazy—what can I tell you?"

"Crazy? How crazy can he be?"

Lenny shows him. He screeches a wild bird call into the mouthpiece and Artie splits a gut.

"Hey look man—I'll call you back. I'll—"

And the two of them let out with the Lone Ranger and Tonto riding off into the *Rosamunda Overture*.

CHAPTER 29

HE CAN'T LIVE WITH THIRTY PERCENT? LET HIM COME on down and see the business Lenny's dragging in. He'll find a way. Let him see the extra tables they've had to crowd together. Let him listen to the rhythm of the cash register as they drink and dig the *shticks*. And if he can't find a way, somebody else will, man, lemme tell you—somebody else will.

Mr. Kelly's. Chicago: I am of Semitic background. I assume I'm Jewish. A lot of Jews who think they're Jewish are not—they're switched babies. Now, a Jew, dictionary-style, is one who is descended from the ancient tribes of Judea, or one who is regarded to have descended from that tribe. But you and I know what a Jew is—ONE WHO KILLED OUR LORD! I don't know if we got much press on that here on the West Coast. This all happened about two thousand years ago, and although there should be a statute of limitations on the crime, we're still paying the

111

dues. Why do you keep busting our balls for this crime?

TRIBUNAL VOICE: Why, Jew? Because you skirt the issue. You blame it on Roman soldiers.

LENNY: All right. I'm gonna clear the air once and for all, and confess. We did it. I did it, my family. We found a note in the basement. It said: "We killed him. Signed, Morty."

You know a lot of people say to me, "Why did you kill Christ?" You wanna know why? We killed him because he didn't want to become a doctor. Actually it's just as well we nailed him when we did. If we'd done it within the last fifty years we'd have had to contend with a generation ·of parochial school kids running around with little gold electric chairs around their necks.

And the mascara's running down the Revloned cheeks. The guys are tinky tinkying into their percale underwear and afterwards a tweedy journalist takes his stenographer's pad into Lenny's dressing room and tells him he seems to have a great deal of social impact.

Two weeks later Lenny finds out this sweet-talking tweedy fellow's John Graham and that he's skewered Lenny in *Time*. Terrific, it's all grist for Lenny's act.

He holds up a copy of the article.

Sick comic Lenny Bruce whose jokes about President Eisenhower, blah, blah, blah—Lenny's off, putting down the magazine. Sick? I'll tell you what's sick. Zsa Zsa Gabor will get sixty-thousand green ones for one week in Vegas and a school teacher in Nevada? Top salary: six thousand for a whole year. Now that's the kind of sick *Time* might write about. Or how about that married guys have to jack off more than anybody else—isn't that weird? All over the country guys are lying on bathroom floors chipping away with Miss December. Why? Because their old ladies don't want to "touch it" anymore and they're too scared to "cheat." Did you know that you can't stop masturbating gradually? Nope. You've got to do it "cold jerky." Now I wonder what *Time* is going to say about that? Lenny Bruce the moralist—right? Wrong. You know if I were as clean and pure as I let on I'd be donating my salary to those school teachers instead of being up here grabbing for number one—right?

Yeah. You know it's weird. I used to get fired for doing bits about guys jacking off. Now I'm getting a following. I mean, is that far out? Oh, here's a bit (again he flips through the magazine). Integration. Well, actually I have some guilts that I don't do enough for integration. You know they asked me to make the marches with them, but I couldn't make the scene 'cause it's always the same old crap— Ray Charles bumping into Little Stevie Wonder all day long. Yeah, really the end. Hey—you don't have to applaud. It's enough. You're sitting there. You're listening.

Hey, you know it's really weird. Everything that strikes me funny is based on all this destruction— this despair and all. But, you know, if the whole world were well, tranquil and all, without the violence? I mean, comeon—where would I be? I'd be standing on an unemployment line somewhere. Like I say, I'm a hustler. As long as they give, I'll grab.

CHAPTER 30

"SO LET'S SEE." THE INTERVIEWER IS BACK TO HONEY again. Honey with the dog and the dirty hair of no particular color.

"While all this was happening for Lenny—*Time* magazine, standing room only—you were in prison?"

"Yeah."

"Did he ever visit you?"

"Oh, yeah—when we could. And uh—well, we wrote to each other a lot."

"What kind of letters?" and Honey starts to look for them in that big cardboard box she's packed her life into. She looks and looks—as if it made any difference.

"Oh shit—well, it's here somewhere, but—well they were like—About how sorry we both were an' all. I don't know. I guess. I guess I never really thought of us as divorced."

The smell of juniper is everywhere. There's a breeze and except for the wall in the background you could

114

think you were anywhere. Except Terminal Island. Where Honey's beautiful red hair has been cut so short Lenny can see her ears.

"I didn't even know you had them, baby."

"Gee, it's good to see you, Len. How are you? You know what? I've been reading about you in the magazines."

"I suppose you gotta. I mean you need'm an all. Everybody needs em."

"Lenny?"

"Your ears, baby. Anybody ever tell you you got dynamite ears?"

Without knowing, he knows she's kept every letter. That she's folded them over and over so many times they're only hanging together out of sheer stubbornness. He'd watched through the iron mesh as they searched her. As the big bulldaggers got their kicks running their hands down her shrunken figure, lost somewhere under that no-color *shmatah* they've hung on her. He couldn't look. It was killing him.

And then there are halls and locks and more searching and more uniforms. For a half an hour it seemed they went over her till they got to go outside and have their "visiting day" picnic.

"It's probably cold," he says, unwrapping the pizza.

"Yeah," she says and takes hold of his sleeve.

"Really boss threads," she whispers and turns her head away so he can't see her eyes. That's when he turns his head away to look like he's having a hard time with the mushy pork.

She picks up an album with Lenny's picture on the front of it. She keeps looking at it and then at him.

"Rab-el-ais. Aris-toph-a—who? Lenny? Who are they, these guys they compare you to here? A couple of drag queens?"

"On the mark, baby."

He looks at her and laughs. What was it about that face on her, he couldn't shake loose—

"You hate it, right?"

"What?"

"My hair. I look like a 'collaborator'!"

"You look like *goyisha punim*, baby, like always."
And again they look away.

"Oh here—I brought you some way-out pictures of Kitty. But you gotta wipe your hands first. They're the best pictures I ever took, you can even see her face —and I don't want you *schmutzing* them up."

"What a *yenta* you are, Lenny."

"*Balabusta*, baby, how many times I gotta—"

"Oh Lenny, they're boss! Can I have them?"

"Sure, you can have them."

"Lenny, does she remember me? Hey never mind. Forget it, pass me the soy sauce."

And it gets very silent.

"So?"

"Yeah. So—"

"I hear you're really swinging out there, Lenny."

"You believe that shit?"

"Yeah. Yeah, I believe it."

She smiles, he smiles back. He passes her some pizza.

"You know, they've cited me for 'meritorious behavior.' Impressed?"

He takes her hand and strokes it.

"I keep it up and they could knock seventy-six days off my time."

He nods.

Honey looks down at her knees and pushes away the uneaten food. It's congealed into a cabbagy gelatin with a thin film of soy sauce that runs off at the edges.

"It must be wonderful to be like, a star and everything Lenny. Like gettin' high, huh?"

And how come, she's still the only one who's always right on target even though she never even got near the shooting gallery—

CHAPTER 31

IT'S LATE WHEN HE GETS HOME. HOME? WHERE he's staying. Wherever the medicine cabinet is. The neat medicine cabinet where everything's up and up. He's got an orthopedist writing script. A druggist with a heart of solid opium. He's legal, baby. Don't hassle him.

Seeing Honey's dragged him. He can't shake her. He can't make it with her. He looks at the kid, he sees Honey. He doesn't look at the kid and he's guilty.

Sally's around his neck. She's on the phone. She's down at the club. He can't cut it. All of them hanging off his ass sucking for something.

He stands in front of the mirror coming down from the uppers he's had to make the scene with Honey. Outside there, the bastards they don't give him an inch. The word's out that he's trouble. They don't like the way he talks. The man's beginning to hang around. Numbers, dealing, international sharking, that's O.K., but now, whenever he goes out or comes in, there they are with the notebooks, with the plainclothesman, maybe he'll make a mistake and buy from somebody who's not so legal; maybe he'll trip over the mike cord again and they'll get him for creating a public nuisance.

Until they bust him for real.

For possession.

"What possession? Man. I got neuritis, call my doctor. I got neuritis and he writes me script."

And they called his doctor. And he was back at work without missing a show. But from then on, every minute, there they were, in their blues—in their raincoats. They'd begun watching Lenny Bruce like he was a communicable disease.

Cops must be half the house, when he comes into the room so high on mad, on, what is this, I'm allava-sudden on the ten most wanted list?

He's mad all right. Those damned bulls sitting there with their notebooks and that way they have of waiting till you spill just one bean. And mad 'cause it was a downer being on nothing, playing it close to the chest, the cops too close for comfort. Waiting around with their empty collars and that look in their grins.

He stands at the mike telling the club owner to "cool it," with his eyes.

"Easy for you to talk 'cool it,'" he looks back. "I got a living to make here. A lot of investment, take it easy, don't give them no beef."

Who? Lenny? as he picks up the night's paper and starts thumbing through it to give the folks a rundown on the day's shockers.

"Now dig it, here's a dandy: an editorial about those teachers who were busted for HOMOSEXUALITY." (He spells it. No one should get shocked.) "Blah blah blah" he reads, "and let us make certain that these sexual deviates are never again allowed inside a classroom again" Psheww. Now that's wrong!

He puts down the paper and looks into the gaggle of eyes he can't see 'cause the light's in his.

And lemme tell you why it's wrong. First of all, they were busted for what they were doing fifteen miles away from the school. O.K.? But more important, what came out at the trial was that they're damned good teachers—and lemme tell you something else. There wasn't one incident reported where a kid came home and said, "Today in school we had five minutes of geography and ten minutes of cocksucking." Not one incident—

The club owner looks around the room. Lenny, he just keeps right on going. He's into the kid who's been sniffing airplane glue for the past six months.

See—so his mother gets hip and she flips out, right?

The audience is cool. Everything's proceeding, except he sees a big blue in the corner writing everything down in a little pad. He's got an orange juice in front of him and he doesn't look up ever. He's just writing and writing.

So she grabs the kid, see, and she says, "Tell me the truth. Are you hooked?" "Nah Ma," he says—"I'm stuck."

And everybody laughs. Everybody but the bull with writer's cramp. He's gotten up, gone to the back of the club and is just waiting till Lenny's through, so he can arrest him again.

This time for Obscenity.
The Jazz Workshop.
1961—
Five years till D. Day.

119

CHAPTER 32

"HEY LENNY." BIG COP. HAND ON LENNY'S ARM.

"Comere Lenny, the Sergeant says he wants I should bring you down to the station house."

"Again?" It was getting to be a number. Do a show, get arrested, get bailed out, do another show—

"What's it this time?" he wants to know. Ever since the last bust he's so clean, he could sing TV soap commercials.

"What makes you think you got a right to use a word like that in a public place?"

"What word, officer? I said a lot of words."

And then there's another cop. The first one puts on the cuffs. The second one moves him over into the squad car.

"You said a lot of crap, buddy."

"Tsktsktsk," Lenny shakes his head. "Gonna haveta wash your mouth out with *Fels Naptha* you talk like that, officer, and you still didn't tell me what I said."

"You know what you said, smart boy."

"I got it all down in here, so don't worry about it.

You think you can go around saying that anyplace you want? It's against the law."

"I didn't do it or anything—I just said it."

"Don't get smart, buddy. You ever said that in front of my wife or kids, I'd flatten you."

"Look man, I don't wanna get emotionally involved."

Still they brought him in, booked him, took his prints, mugged him, got his social security number and then The People of the State of California took him to court.

For the first time.

Before Judge Axelrod, who was, according to Lenny, really distinguished looking.

He looked like a movie judge, like Andy Hardy's father—right? So naturally he'll be cool. He'll give me a break. He'll be kind, good to children. You know, Andy Hardy's father—

Except that pretty soon things got pretty hairy.

When the interviewer talked to Sally about it, she said he started slipping bits about his arrest into his act.

The interviewer asked her if she thought he enjoyed it . . .

"Well, I don't know," she said. "It's just that it interfered with his act."

Honey said she thought at first he really did enjoy it.

"You know, at first he got a lot of publicity."

Artie said, "Enjoyed it? Hell, no. He became obsessed with it—anyway towards the end."

'Cause that trial was really the beginning of the end for Lenny. Not that he didn't go on another five years. But it's just that this was only the second arrest and how many people want to pay a cover charge to hear a lot of legal mumbo jumbo.

If it pleased the court.

Writs of this and that.

Continuances.

Transcripts.

They came to hear funny Lenny. And sometimes he wasn't, that's all. Sometimes he had other things on his mind.

And then the proceedings got harder for Lenny to follow. The courtroom stuff. It got technical. And the nice warm-hearted judge got testy. The witnesses and lawyers began to define the different kinds of public places. A station house as against a college classroom as compared with a club like *The Jazz Workshop*.

And what if there were children present?

But, Lenny's lawyer says, "If it please the court—no children were present."

And all of a sudden Lenny's opened his yap.

"Your honor, even if they *were* present—" That's the point. I mean like the nights when he talked at the club about what obscene really means . . . Like a teacher who makes six thousand for a whole year's work and Zsa Zsa Gabor, who gets that for showing her tits for one half an hour. What's the matter with sucking somebody's cock? He wouldn't care if Kitty heard.

"Will you please let me do this my way?" his lawyer yells at him.

And then the judge gets in on the act.

"Young man, you'd better let your attorney try this case. As far as I'm concerned, I'm ready to find you guilty right now." Then he turns to the lawyer, one educated man to another.

"However," he says in that hoary judgy way they have, "I will grant a continuance as you've requested."

"Now it is my understanding that you've got a show Sunday," he says to Lenny. "I want to caution you right now, young man, that if I get a report that

122

you repeated any of this language, any of these words, you will take the consequences. Is that clear?"

"If I repeat *what* words specifically, your Honor?"

Did you ever see a mad judge? Baby, he looked down at Lenny like a Doberman pinscher at a crippled chipmunk.

"You say *anything* that is obscene," he hissed, turning the color of incensed judges, "and I'll take it into consideration when I finally dispose of this case."

Exit: Andy Hardy's father.

And Lenny's back to the *Workshop*. The word has been out for how many hours? Didja hear what happened to Lenny?

Those SOBs.

Those cocksuckers.

And the place is mobbed.

Auerbach's in heaven. They've sold more Johnny Walker Black in three-quarters of an hour than all last week. And they're still coming. He thinks to himself: imagine if they could only book Judge Axelrod. He smiles.

"Bless you, bless you—"

Lenny's coming in, arms upraised. The faithful are faithful; the healer heals. He takes the mike from the stand and then blesses them again.

"Because you're good. Good!" and then he shields his eyes from the spots.

"Wow! Look at all that Blue. Is there anyone out there that's *not* a policeman? Ah—I uh, seem to be under a little pressure tonight to cool my act."

Everybody laughs. They snicker and they poke their sidekicks. It's Lenny and them, baby. And ain't it cozy.

"See I was arrested on this stage a few nights ago for saying a let's see—an eleven-letter word, which was used in the context of defending a certain homosexual practice. I'm not going to repeat the word tonight, but—it starts with a *c* and ends with a *g*. Now *they* said it was a favorite homosexual practice, which is weird, 'cause I don't relate that word to homosexuals.

It relates to any woman I know or would know or would love or would marry. But they got hung up with faggotry. All right—"

All right—they're with him.

"We're with you," they say. They lean forward in their chairs and show their capped teeth.

"Look their whole scene was that Dirty Lenny said a dirty word."

Was he telling them? His people?

"So anyway. I'd like to ask you a few questions." They lean even closer.

"How many people in this club tonight have ever used that word—blah-blah-blah."

Well, this is the big laff-a-meter moment. The time the chaff gets cut from the bait. The hands are raised in formation. It's the least, Lenny. The very least.

"Cool. O.K. Now let's get really honest. You sir, have you ever had your blah blahhed?"

Which is when the chaff begins to start separating pretty fast. After all, it's one thing when you're raising your hand with the company of legions. Still, the guy's cool. Maybe he doesn't come out and say so but he's smiling. He's really smiling.

"Did you dig it?"

And again with a smile. A real toothpaste ad.

"The stuff of the hero, man." Lenny gives him the twenty-one-gun click of the heels and then looks way out there behind the lights.

"O.K., how many other guys in this room have had their blah blahhed?" The judge ought to be there— not an obscene word all night.

Six, maybe eight hands in the air, but not one cop. Lenny gives one the stare.

"Comeon now officer—you're under oath remember," and his people are getting their own back.

Then when he's milked the moment to its climax he moves on.

"O.K. Lady, what about you? Did you ever blah a blah?"

Oh boy, does she do a freeze. She looks at the soles on her shoes and waits for Samson to pull out the pillars. Nevermind, the guy with her breaks out a big affirmative nod, and the crowd goes bananas, which in some circles is really an obscene word.

"Hey, I don't think the officers over there could see that," Lenny crows. "See, Officer, she went like this—" and he shakes his head, "no"—"and he went like this—" and he shakes his head "yes." He's breaking up.

"Believe me— this time the whole audience gets *shlepped* away." They're laughing and he's shaking his head.

"You know, I think I'm doing the dirtiest show in my life. Now, if anyone here has found this obscene, then you're full of blah, and I hope you never get your blah blahhed again."

He's pulled it off.

The audience thinks Lenny Bruce is the funniest, most outrageous cat in the business.

Judge Axelrod thinks he's guilty as charged.

The next night, Lenny quotes him, back at the *Workshop*.

"The cat finds me guilty and I get sentenced to one year in jail and one thousand dollars fine, but don't get shook up on my account, *tzotzkelehs*. We made a motion for a jury trial and the show goes on. Lissen, twelve 'average' members of our community can better determine what's obscene—right? Better than one judge who looks like Andy Hardy's father and turns out to be Barten McClain. I mean, tell me if I'm wrong —right?"

CHAPTER 33

AND THE TRIAL DOES GO ON WITH THE TWELVE PEERS.
Lenny's getting a lot of material for his act. (Some
saying he's getting the only material for his act. Forget it with the Scottsboro Shaft, Lenny. How about
The Paladium, Father Flotzky—a lot of his "regulars"
could go with a little of his old *shticks* once in a while.
Not *only* a rundown of what Officer Ryan said that
day in court. How the Defense handled him and then
what the DA came back with. It wasn't always funny,
Lenny, and that's what it's all about, fella—we pays
our money, you deliver the punchlines.)

OFFICER RYAN: I was told by my immediate superior
that the show at this club was of a lewd nature and
that I should go in and see the show and find out
what the complaint was all about.

'Cause if Lenny's act were proved lewd that would
involve the statute on "community standards." "O.K.,"
says Lenny's lawyer, there's an opening. "Tell me,

Officer Ryan, what would you say is the nature of that particular community? Isn't it true that three doors down, there are female impersonators grinding away in what might be referred to as 'scanty' attire? Men in women's pasties?

"And what about the *Moulin Rouge* where they run stripping contests for housewives, so the ladies at home can see just how good they can shake it without breaking it? Is that your professional idea of good clean family entertainment?"

And so much for the community. Point: Lenny; which brings his lawyer to the eleven-letter illegal word itself.

QUESTION: Tell me, Officer, the word in question. It is frequently used around the police station, is it not?

OBJECTION.

THE COURT: Well, a police station, of course, is a public place.

ANSWER: I have heard it used.

QUESTION: You laughed at Lenny Bruce's performance, did you not?

ANSWER: No, I didn't.

QUESTION: Did you observe whether the audience was laughing?

ANSWER: Yes, I did.

QUESTION: Were they?

ANSWER: At times, yes.

QUESTION: And nobody made any complaint to you, though you were in uniform?

ANSWER: No. No one.

QUESTION: Officer Ryan, have you ever used the word —cocksucker?

ANSWER: Not that I can remember.

QUESTION: You are quite familiar with the term "cocksucker," are you not?

ANSWER: I've heard it used—yes.

QUESTION: As a matter of fact, the word "cocksucker"

127

is frequently used in the police station, is it not?

DA: That's irrelevant and immaterial, if your Honor please. What's used—

JUDGE: The objection is overruled. You may answer, Officer.

COP: Could I hear the question again, please.

The clerk reads the question. He reads as if he's going over this week's laundry list.

CLERK: As a matter of fact the word "cocksucker" is frequently used in the police station, is it not?

COP: I have heard it used—yes.

DEFENSE ATTORNEY: Yes, you have heard the term "cocksucker" used in a police station, which is a public place.

And Lenny turns to the lawyer next to him and goes ape.

"They're all getting off on that word, will you lissen to them?"

At which point Lenny's lawyer gets around to Lenny's place in the literary hierarchy.

He said that Lenny's performance related intimately to the kind of social satire to be found in the works of such great authors as Aristophanes, and Jonathan Swift, and all of that.

The prosecutor then objected because Aristophanes wasn't going to be testifying at the trial.

Then Lenny's lawyer said to the judge that he wasn't going to call Mr. Aristophanes to the stand and the judge said,

"I don't think you could, very well," and Lenny cracked up again.

But then the testimony got more and more technical—no easy victories yet. They started in on the Penal Code. Police Section 176 where obscene language is defined as "indecent, immoral, impure, bawdy" and etc.

And then back to the word again. The word, the

word. Lenny's dying. These guys are really getting their rocks off on it. Lenny works up a routine . . .

THE DA: The guy said blah-blah-blah! I'm not gonna lie to you. He said it. It's in the minutes. He's glad he said blah-blah-blah!

THE JUDGE: He said blah-blah-blah?

BAILIFF: He said it. Blah-blah-blah—that's what the man said.

It's getting blurry, time in court. Time out.
And then on to the witnesses.

DEFENSE ATTORNEY: Now, Reverend Mooney—how would you characterize Mr. Bruce's work?

The Reverend speaks in a quiet reverend-type way.

MOONEY: Well, to me he is a sort of comic Shaman.

Except the DA can't hear him, and tells him so.

MOONEY: (Louder, but still reverent.) He is a sort of comic Shaman—a man who stands in front of his tribe and exorcises the taboos of his tribe by mocking them.

DA: Louder, please, Reverend. (He knows this bird. Some reverend. Down at the cuckoo's place of perdition, anything goes, talk about dirty? Judson Church, the way *they* carry on??)

MOONEY: I'm sorry. He exorcises the taboos of the tribe by bringing them out into the open and in doing so, releases the people from their fear of the taboos.

And where the defendant sits, some of his tribe see that he sits very still, but kisses his own hand.

So far it's a picnic.

Realities are getting more and more mixed up. Lenny's time on stage and in court are fusing. One feeds the other. He wants to redo "bits" on the witness stand 'cause he would have done them a little differently. What went on Tuesday 10-1, 3-5, he did Tuesday night 9-10, 11-12.

9

DA: Now, officer. What was the nature of this "chant"?

COP: It was a chant that—well, it was supposed to be talk between a man and a woman who were involved in a perverse act.

Perverse? As the judge raps the gavel and the same audience who heard Lenny last night at the club quiet down in court. The material is aired over and over. Lenny gets a chance to see how it goes down in front of stenographers, the bailiffs, the cops off duty, the cops on—Lenny's started taping everything—what he said, what she said, what he did on stage. What the DA said in court. Pretty soon nothing is said anywhere that isn't preserved, played back and replayed back later.

Now a drum solo I've heard my whole adult life and as a kid when they thought I was sleeping. To is a preposition. Come is a verb. To is a preposition. Come is a verb. The verb intransitive. To come. To come. Yeah—

(In the club he plays on a drum. It doesn't come in too well over the tape.)

Too cuuum. Tooo cuuuum. It's been like a big drum solo. Did you come? Dijacome? Didjacumgood, didjacumgoooood? Dijacumgood didjacumgooddidjacumgood? I come better with you sweetheart than anyone in the whole damn world.

(The judge is getting very annoyed.)

Goddamn I sure do love you. I come good with you but I come too quick, don't I? That's 'cause I love ya so goddamn much.

And some dude in the back of the spectator's rows is sneezing into his hand. The judge is turning maroon. He raps the gavel again.

"Now turn that thing off a moment. Now I won't have it. I have admonished this court before. This is a very serious question involved here."

That dude who laughed back there—twenty years of hard questions.

The court comes back to order. The tape recorder is once again set in motion.

Yeah, if you just wouldn't say don't come in me—that's what does it. That's what makes me come so quick. Don't come in me don't come in me don't come in me mimme mimme—(he sings) I can't come, don't ask me—(He speaks) 'Cause you don't love me, that's why. What the hell's loving you got to do with it. I can't come because I drank too damn much. Now, if anybody in this room finds those two words, to come, objectionable—if they make you uncomfortable, if you think I'm rank for saying them—then you probably can't come.

And forget it. Everybody's busting one gut or another.

"Mr. Bruce, you're smiling," the judge sputters. "This is not for your entertainment. I want to say something—and this is off the record—"

He pauses and wipes his mouth with the carefully ironed handkerchief his wife sees he keeps for just such emergencies.

"I've been on the bench for twenty years, and I have *never* had to listen to such filth."

"Your honor—Do you believe in God?"

"Sit down, Mr. Bruce. Please—Just sit down."

"Look, if you believe there is a God—a God who made your body—then why do you keep telling little children to 'cover up, cover up,' that the body is dirty, the titties are vulgar? Because if the body is dirty then the fault lies with the manufacturer, so you've got to *shlep* God into court along with me." Which made a couple of points for the judge, if you asked a few of the *Workshop*'s customers when Lenny repeated the bit on stage that night.

"Comeon, Harry. You know—sometimes this Bruce

131

goes a little too far, wouldn't you say? *God?*"

"Where's your sense of humor? At least he gave him top billing."

And then back to Section 311.6 of the California Penal Code which states: Any person who knowingly speaks any obscene song, ballad or other words in a public place is guilty of a misdemeanor, all of which is then explained to the jury by the judge.

"Now," he starts, giving his best profile the Southern Exposure.

"Obscene means to the 'average person,' applying contemporary standards of the community. The dominant appeal of the matter being to arouse prurient interest—which is defined as a morbid or shameful interest in nudity, sex or excretion which goes substantially beyond the limits of such matters and is matter that is utterly without social importance."

Got that Charlie?

Except he's not through by half.

"Now—sex and obscenity are not synonymous."

And on this note Lenny shakes his head and smiles disbelievingly.

"In order to make sex obscene it is necessary that the portrayal of it must be done in such a way that its dominant tendency is to corrupt the average adult by creating a clear and present danger of antisocial behavior." And Lenny's taking notes like mad.

That night he further interprets the judge for his audience.

"You see maybe some guy'll see my show and get so horny he'll go to the museum and jerk off a dinosaur."

This feat he demonstrates by making a hoop of his arms and then furiously rubbing them back and forth several times.

And then finally,

Finally,

Finally—

All the evidence is in.

All the explanations and explanations of explanations are in. The jury has gone out and the jury has come back. They are ready with their verdict.

The court is tense. It's a toss-up as to who is more interested in the verdict, Lenny or the judge. Both edge forward on their chairs. Eternities—hyper-ventilation, and then the foreman hands the little piece of paper to the court clerk who reads with great solemnity:

"We the jury find the defendant 'Not Guilty.'"

Defeat and Exultation at the same fell swoop.

But then, as they say, the last race is never run until the horse drops dead.

CHAPTER 34

"NO," HONEY TOLD THE INTERVIEWER. SHE'D GOTTEN up and started to walk around. Quickly. From one side of the room to the other. Then she started to talk fast too, as if to get over this part without having to remember it.

"I got in some trouble, so I had to serve my full time."

"What kind of trouble?"

"Well—I just did something crazy."

He waited for her to finish. To tell him what.

She didn't.

"Anyway, you finally got out—"

"Yeah. You know, they give you a lot of speeches about rehabilitation. They lay a little bread on you. Sure—they try and help and all. Then—they drop you on the sidewalk and there you is."

Two years is a long time, especially for a woman. That's what Sally had said to Lenny about Honey's sentence. Which wasn't telling half of it. As the bus with the lettering, DEPARTMENT OF CORRECTION, pulled to a stop and the two bewildered women stepped out into the daylight, it might as well have been twenty.

Honey had changed. And it wasn't just the hair. Or the dress. The figure that's lost inside an out-of-date, too-garish rag that had somehow, in her mind, been seen as what? Sexy? Was that Honey's old image? It no longer seemed valid.

She's so bony. The large frame jutting out of skin that had once curved around her, like a Minneapolis milkmaid. Except that that wasn't it either. A couple of malteds could put on curves in a hurry. It was the expression. The eyes, the lines etched into the mouth. "It's over," written with an inner stylus in the way she moved, in how she glanced around her, in the lost hunch to her shoulders.

The other girl waved at her faintly. Her family sat in a pickup truck across the avenue. They hadn't gotten out of the car to meet her, but at least they were there.

Honey looked around almost furtively. There was nobody there to meet her and she knew it.

I'm divorced, I'm divorced, she told herself as she walked down the street avoiding the cracks in the sidewalk. Keep saying it, Honey, get a grip on your expectations. You're divorced. Your kid doesn't know you. You've had two years in the hole and what are you good for?

Get used to it, man. You're pushing thirty, you're long since over Hot Honey Harlow. You're a broad, baby—nothing but an old beat-up, used-up, junkie broad. You wouldn't bring two bucks as a Chinatown hooker. And she leaned up against the telephone booth and had the dry sobs. No tears, just a wracking holding back. What was there to cry over? Did she actually think he'd come?

Without looking in her bag, she knew the number. And that struck her as futile too. Her one big accomplishment in life—she always knew Lenny's number.

"I am sorry, the number you have dialed is no longer in service. If you wish further assistance, please dial the operator."

That's when the tears came.

"What am I going to do, Lenny?? Lenny???? What am I going to do?"

"Hey lady—if you're not going to use the phone, wouldya mind letting—"

She turned around as if hit. Turned around and there he was—Lenny! The sportscar parked on the street with the motor still running. Lenny, in black. Nehru jacket, black jeans, black eyes—Lenny, Lenny, Lenny.

"I thought you weren't going to—"

"Come?" he said and laughed. "Now you know, baby, that's never been one of my problems," and all of a sudden it seemed like Honey again. The two of them riding down the freeway, Honey swivelled around on her hips so she didn't miss a word, so she could reach out and touch him. Feel the tops of his hands as he drove. Get the excitement of his voice as he told her and told her—

"Yeah, sure—I was relieved, but you know, that verdict had nothing to do with you know, what I thought—Justice, right—Remember the chick I told you about?"

"The one in the flowered dress?"

"Yeah. Stella Dallas. Well, she was the one, all right. She got in the jury room and had them all locked up, bitchin', bitchin', bitchin'. 'He's guilty, the SOB, ram it to him, who does he think he is' and all that shit—but then, all of a sudden she falls over and plays dead: 'O.K. he's not guilty.' " "How come?"

(How come, Lenny, I love you, I'm so glad you came. Stay with me, Lenny, I need you, I don't know what I would have done if you hadn't—)

"You're gonna *plotz* from this baby. Dig it—she's

a lush. Could you live? The bitch hadda get the hell outta there to get herself a drink. And that's justice for ya."

"Because she was a—Oh Lenny, that's wild."

"Yeah, dig it, I was saved by Gallo Wine."

"Well, anyway, you beat it."

"Yeah, I beat it. But, you know, I had hoped to really win something. You know, the merits of the thing and all. My Constitutional guarantees. See, the First Amendment—"

Sure, sure, whatever you say, baby.

"You know about the First Amendment?"

"Not exactly."

"Free speech. You see—"

"I'm for free speech, Daddy," and she can't control herself any longer. She leans over and kind of wraps herself around him.

"I love you, Daddy. Where we going?"

He knew she was going to ask that. He signaled into the left lane.

"You're gonna love it, baby. I, ah—I found this great apartment for you. It's got—"

"You mean we're not gonna be together?" And, like that, the haunted dog look comes back to her eyes. There's a very small wince that neither of them notice. That both notice.

"Well, we'll be close, it's like a—ten-minute drive from my house."

She moves very slowly back onto her own seat again.

"Look, Honey, I've given this a lot of thought, you know—I mean I really think it's for the best. I'm working, I've got these wacky hours and—"

"Lenny, it's not like the old days, I've really cleaned up. I mean I don't even smoke anymore, I mean cigarettes—And I'm really gonna stay clean. You know—and oh Lenny, I've missed you so much. I—"

She looks out of the window. "And—Kitty—"

Her voice trails off.

"Boy, lookit the smog."

Later too she tries to keep telling herself "I'm divorced, I'm divorced," but all the time Lenny points out this and that feature in the apartment: the hifi, the sofa bed, the kitchenette, the new clothes he's bought her, it's no use. She don't wanna hear, man —she don't wanna hear.

Anyway, she adjusted. In her way.

Wednesday she called Marty. He wasn't home.

Thursday Freak Harrison. They called him Freak because of the way he—"you know," she said. And if Lenny didn't exactly know for sure, he got the message.

By Friday she was prepared to go over and see Kitty.

Kitty who was already going to school.

"Gowan over and give your momma a big kiss," Gramma Sally said.

"Momma?"

"Don't tell me the cat's gotcha tongue, Kitchycoocoo." Sometimes Gramma Sally called her Kitchycoocoo. Kitty called Gramma Grammagoodle.

"Gowan—your ma's been away a long time. She missed you."

Only it was no different than if Honey had been any one of a million other babes who wandered in and out of the Bruce menagerie. So Honey went on home and called up Marty again.

"Yeah?"

"Marty remember me, it's Honey."

"Honey who?"

"Bruce—Honey Bruce."

"Bruce? Oh yeah—Honey? Hey, there Honey, what's shakin' baby?"

"Everything."

"So you're out, huh?"

"Yeah—so I'm out."

"So where are you?"

"Around the corner. I'm here, man—*Hullehvuud!* Got a real nice pad."

"Outa sight."

"Yeah—Lenny had it put together for me. A real heavy pad."

"Is he there? Lenny?"

"Just a minute, I'll check out the terlet. Nope—'pears like I'm all alone."

"Well, maybe I'll fall by later? Anyplace special?"

"1401-½ Havenhurst."

"See you."

She starts to hang up the phone and then stops.

"Oh, ah—Marty—Why don't you bring over a little—?"

"Sure, sure baby, but wheeew, let's not tee-iz-awk about it on the phee-iz-own, O.K.?"

"Oh yeah—O.K."

"Later."

"Soon as you can, Marty. Soon as you can."

"Yeah, baby. Yeah."

While Lenny got famouser and famouser: "the comic with the sewer mouth."

Who all the "in" people went to see because maybe he'd get arrested, and it was all so socially unjust, entertaining and mod. The elegants. In their *Yves St. L's* and their cool.

"All right, funny man—amuse me."

The uptown bunch, evicting the turtleneck crowd. The skin-deep hipsters.

"But lissen," Artie said, "he changed a lot too, you know. Coming on like a rabbi, with his seek-me-and-ye-shall-find shit. The *meshugeneh* Messiah, Lenny—only sometime, you know, even he didn't know the difference."

Look—I'm not anti-Christ *or* anti-religion, I just think it's encouraging that large numbers of people are leaving the churches and going back to God.

Clap, clap, titter. Sounds of long fingernails and Patou.

They're with him, and some of the old bunch too.

The perennial sweet young doe in the front who only wants a touch of his hemline.

"You're the truth, Lenny. You are really the truth."

"A nut!" he says. But she's right.

You're all right. Come, get the word, lay some more of that sweet bread my way.

You know, it's always fascinated me. We live in a society that is very strict about its concepts of what is "clean" and what is "dirty." You'd think, wouldn't you, that the entertainment capital of such a society would be the *most* austere. O.K., so what's the main attraction in Las Vegas?

Well, uh—at the *Stardust* we have the Passion Play.

Correct; then they're consistent. What follows the Passion Play?

Well, I think they're having a Monet exhibit, then Eugene Ormandy and the New York City Ballet. It's a very spiritual type of show.

Is that the attraction that all the purists support in Las Vegas? Uh uh—I'll tell you what's the attraction: Tits and ass.

I beg your pardon?

Ah, tits and ass, that's what the attraction is.

Just tits and ass?

Oh, no—an Apache team and tits and ass.

Well, what's the second biggest attraction?

More tits and ass.

Get off it. Do you mean to tell me that *Life* magazine would devote three full pages to tits and ass?

Yup—right next to the article by Billy Graham and Norman Vincent Peale. *Life* and *Look* and *Nugget* and *Rogue* and *Dude* and *Cavalier* and *Swank* and *Gent* and *Pageant* (The Legion of Decency's *Playboy*) and all those other stroke books. *National Geographic* with those African chicks—Oh yeah, they're all stroke books.

"He's so devastatingly right," said one pace-setting

jet-lagger to another. His chic counterpart moved his lips imperceptibly. It was, for him, an ovation.

At the end of the bar, the cognoscenti who stood to avoid the cover snickered at the smart set.

Under the blinking GENTS a pimpled trio, sipping Cokes and gorging on Mars bars, nodded; and a short man with a wrinkled IQ said to a tweed lady with 80/90 vision and an Etruscan nose: "You see what I mean about the Melville allegory, don't you?"

Everybody was buying pieces of Lenny. Everybody saw, whatever light they saw, through another knothole. Everybody wanted to be part of the phenomenon.

You know it would take a lot of tension out of crap like the Bay of Pigs or the Cuban missile thing if we could just picture JFK in the White House bathroom wacking it to Miss July once in a while.

Ah, well and good, but you still can't just put "Tits and Ass Nightly" up on the marquee. It's dirty. And it's vulgar.

Not to me, Jim. I like to hug 'em and kiss 'em. But O.K., if the words get to you I'll change it to: "*Tuchushes* and *Nay-Nays* Nightly."

Hmmmm, that's a little better.

Not anti-Semitic, eh? Point one for you. But how about making it even more austere—Latin: "*Gluteus Maximus* and *Pectoralis Major* Nightly."

Now that I like. That's clean.

To you, *shmuck*—but it's dirty to the Latins. And just because you're an illiterate doesn't get you off the hook.

At which point the Classics professor's wife, Emma, turned to the Classics professor. "Language is culture; culture is language," she whispered conspiratorially. After all, wasn't that Charles' point? Hadn't Charles been saying that to his classes for years? Now he'd have to admit that this Bruce person was not utterly without social importance, and that her subscription to *The Village Voice* did too have its pulse on the heartbeat of the nation.

> Well, I don't care what you say, you can't just put *Tits and Ass* up there. You have to have something a little—well Parisienne perhaps—Like the Follies? French tits and ass? *Class with Ass?*
>
> Unless, of course, I can have something patriotic. Now—how about *The Most American Girls in the World?* American tits and ass—Grandma Moses' tits and Norman Rockwell's ass: draw my ass and win a Buick. My ass you can draw—

By this time so many people are just flat out laughing, nobody much notices the two cops who have gotten up in back. The one who blocks the door, or the tall patrolman who has worked his way up to the stage and crooks a finger at Lenny.

"Yes? Officer? Can I help you? Ooops—I mean may I—May I help you?"

But they notice now. The Classics professor is glaring at his wife as he has never glared before. The six hipsters in the corner are quietly emptying their pockets on the rugs and the crowd who came to see Lenny get arrested again are finally getting their money's worth.

"O.K., Officer," Lenny's saying to the cop who almost seems apologetic. "That's cool, baby—that's cool. Look, ladies and gentlemen—I'm sorry, but I'm being busted so I can't finish the performance."

Hell, it's their turn now. They stand in outrage. They stomp their feet. They turn to the protectors of their property with expressions of contempt for their lower-class morality—until Lenny picks up the mike again.

"Hey, wait a minute folks—let's just wait a minute. Now that's really unfair. These guys are doing what they're paid to do. What *you* paid them to do. These guys get a hundred bucks a week to get shot at, and the truth of the matter is *you're* the ones who are arresting me. You are. We're the lawmakers, so if you don't dig the laws then you better get hip and change them. Right?"

"Yeah?" as he followed the officer back through the tables to the door and saw how suddenly lots of people had to look down into their screwdrivers, or lean over to get their pennies back into their loafers.

CHAPTER 35

THE INTERVIEWER WANTED TO KNOW ABOUT THE
Troubador Theatre gig in Hollywood. It was 1962,
a year after the *Jazz Workshop* arrest, and that's when
he'd heard, things had really started going belly-up
with Lenny.

"Sure, they changed," Sally said. "I mean who was
he kidding with this lawyer *shtick* of his. He never
even passed ninth grade."

Artie had a two-dollar bill on the subject too.

"Day, night, night, day, and comeon—The customers came for a night's laugh, there was Lenny up
there with the mike giving them case histories, coming on like a law *mavin,* and taking everything down
on the tapes. Everything. I'm telling you the guy taped
his trips to the head, it got that bad."

"And so, my strong feeling is, Al, even though I'm
only a layman, as you so often make clear to me, I
really feel strongly that the following concept be in-

cluded in the defense," he'd tell his lawyer into the recorder, and then repeat to his audience in front of the lights, recording it again.

Lenny seemed to be welding one half of his mind to the electronic ear and the other to Oliver Wendell Cardoza.

"He drove all his friends nuts with it," Artie said. Sally agreed.

"Look, what did he need to bankrupt himself hiring a hundred lawyers if all he was going to do was turn into a bookworm."

"Yeah, he had everybody running up and down the West Coast digging up old lawbooks, case numbers, newspaper clippings—"

"Even Kitty," Sally interrupted. "Instead of reading her *Jack and the Beanstalk,* she'd have to listen to Holmes' decision on Weber vs. Fields."

"No question—the guy was flipping. He'd hire one lawyer Wednesday at 3:00, and by 8:00 at night he'd be on the phone, who else could he get to come in the back door and take over? The place was crawling with lawyers. And the tape mania? This is no crap now— I got the bills in front of me—$63,000 for tape recordings? You know how many good times you can buy with $63,000?"

Troubles.

"And it ain't only the spending of the money. What about earning it. Look, a guy works in your club and talks dirty, O.K.? So they arrest him. Sure, but then maybe they arrest you—or they start with the harassing. Revoking your liquor license, 435 Board of Health violations, you know—And all of a sudden, who wants to hire that guy anymore?"

"So Lenny turned off the outside world with the tape recorder. Right?"

Well, let Lenny tell it.

"See, the whole thing comes down to this prurient interest thing. But look, prurient interest is like the steel interest. What's wrong with appealing to it? We appeal to the *killing* interest—and look Mel, don't tell me it's not germane to my case and I should leave the legalisms to you. It's a point, Melvin."

Enter: Honey.

Lenny looks at her like "Yeah—sure, I know you. If I could only remember from where—"

She reaches out her hand and flips off the tape recorder.

"Whatcha do that for? I'm working."

"Lenny—Lenny, I need some money."

"Oh wow. Great. You need some money. Terrific timing baby. I haven't worked in three weeks. I got four lawyers doing Jose Greco on my checkbook. If you could only hang on—a coupla weeks baby, a—"

"Lenny, I can't wait. I need some money right now. You know—*Now*, Lenny."

"For what?" As if he doesn't know too much already. He looks out of the window and sees the open convertible in the drive. The one Honey's been in nonstop since she got out. Marty's convertible. The shifty Marty. Marty the stock, MGM no good; down to the black shirt, the diamond stickpin and the eighty-five dollar alligator shoes.

"Well, I can see your position baby," and no more questions asked.

Honey watches as he reaches down into his pocket.

"That's really hip," she says, kicking the desk with her pointed toe.

He counts out a couple of bills and then a couple more.

"You don't care what I do or who I do it to? Huh, Lenny?"

Lenny looks up and then can't. He hands her the money and goes back to his desk. She goes to the window, opens it and calls down.

146

"Hey, Marty—Wanna take a swim? Here? 'Mr. Hip' won't care . . . Will you 'Mr. Hip?' "

And Lenny doesn't look up. Either when she slams down the window or when she starts to take her blouse off.

"In addition, I found one or two other things in the case of U.S. vs. Schenck. Now—"

Except that Honey's gotten up on a chair and it's as if the old band is blaring away in the background. She's forgotten the guy in the convertible downstairs. She's forgotten anything but Lenny's eyes and how to steal them back again. She still knows how to take it off so it hurts. She still knows Lenny's gonna put down that big book he has his nose in. She still knows Lenny's gonna get it up like he always did when she took it off. Only it's not so simple now. Now, along with making sure he still has it for her she wants him to police her excesses.

"Tell me when it's enough, Lenny, I'm begging you," down to her panties, down to her spike heels, down to her push-up—

O.K., he was watching her, and waited till she was down to the white flesh that had long since dug itself into his brain where it festered still.

"You sure know how to strip, Lady," he said. But the rest?

"Tell me when it's enough, baby."

That part she was going to have to figure out for herself. No more *Daddy*, baby. No more hold my hand and cross me. She had a baby of her own, if she could get around to it sometime. And so did he.

A simple statement of fact. "You sure know how to strip, Lady," bringing tears of rage to Honey. Rage that somehow couldn't goose him anymore.

"And so—yeah, Justice Holmes said, 'The most stringent protection of free speech would not protect a man in—' "

As she stormed out and slammed the door.

As he watched her wave to that creep Marty she had wrapped around her life those days.

As the two of them slid down into the water of his pool.

"Would not protect a man in falsely shouting 'fire' in a theater causing a panic, which leads us to the case of—"

The sound of his wife. Ex-wife, bitch-wife, splashing in the pool. Sinking to the bottom with her thighs sucking in that bastard. Giggling, splashing—

"The Case of Gitlow vs. People of New York, 268, U.S. 652 (1952) —"
and more sounds and more laughter and Lenny, losing the thread, and then Honey and then Lenny furiously flipping through the thick pages of the book.

"—aahhh, U.S. 652 (1925, 1925) —"

And finally a laugh. A single soft Honey laugh that floats up from the pool and winds its memories about Lenny's throat.

"—the stringent protection of free, of free, of—"

"Marty!" he screams. "Marty!" as he throws the recorder across the room with the back of his hand. As he pauses at the desk long enough to pick up a letter opener and then dashes headlong down the stairs, out the door and towards the pool.

"You bastard. You get your hands off my old lady or I'm gonna tie your cock in a knot—"

Except that the look in his eye was worse. Worse even than quick murder. Limb from slow limb over cauldrons of steaming pain and miseries in that look as Marty jumped bare ass out of that pool before it turned A Positive with his own plasma. Marty into the convertible and gone. Without a "later," for Honey, nookie only after safe and sound, baby. Dig?

And then Honey and Lenny.

Honey calling his name over and over, surrounding him with her everything.

Lenny, he should stop her.

148

Lenny, all she's ever wanted was to do right by him, why doesn't he care anymore?

Lenny, Lenny, Lenny, until they made it and for a while—it was just like old times.

CHAPTER 36

"THAT WAS, MAYBE, THE BEST TIME," HONEY SAID.
The interviewer didn't say anything.
"Lenny felt that way too—I know he did."
Then she started to cry.
"Hey, take it easy."
She kept on sniveling. After a while she said, "But that was always the worst lie of all."
"What's that?"
"The lie that nobody ever believes—the sick junkie lie—that we'd kick, that we could anytime we really wanted to, but never today."

While Lenny played the straight-up, man-of-the-word for her? Honey's, Do-Like-I-Say Guru? Only just don't roll up his sleeves. Because, face it, Lenny spent whatever time he wasn't quoting from this or that law-book, digging the life of the junkie. Looking for a connection and sweating out the good from the shit.

O.K., so some say everything was legal. He had

this neuritis. Pleurisy. Insomnia. Chilblains. Hemorrhoids. Bleeding gums. He was still high, wasn't he? Dig that rhythm, the way he moved through the cities of his life like a cat on a pogo stick. With *shticks,* with games. With a pattern he could no more break than play the Kiwanis circuit.

Not to mention that getting busted, besides being a drain on his life, was big romance. Busted for his mouth. Busted for the tracks up his arteries. In one year and one month he got busted four different times. Two and two. Obscenity and drugs. Strike what and he's out?

It got so lots of people were laying odds. On which death-wish he'd wish on himself harder.

As Dirty Lenny got dirtier. As a lot of folks took a bar of *Lifebuoy* with them when they went—if they went. 'Cause as Lenny got scruffier, the nicer type class of clientele walked out on the tightrope he walked, zonked out of his bloody bird.

And not only the nicer type class of clientele. Even his mother was losing patience.

"For God sake, Lenny, cancel. You can't play a show looking like that! Forcrissakes anybody—anybody with half your brain—If the cops were *hocking* them, they'd clean up their act till they were out of the spotlight. But not *you.* You gotta go out there with a pocket full of dope. Show the bastards—Lenny, for God sakes, cancel already!"

While Lenny, her boy wonder, he falls to one knee and makes his face go Jolson.

"Ah cain't cancel, Maaaamy. De show muss go on," at which point he falls on his face and breaks a couple of blood vessels.

Does a flickering smile pass across Honey's face? Now that he's down, does that bring him back to her again?

Sally things it does.

"He was fine. Then you had to be *shlepped* into it again."

"O.K." she says, taking an eyebrow pencil and drawing dots up and down her arm.

"I'll kill myself."

"You'll kill each other is what'll happen," and the two of them lift Lenny up to a chair while he mumbles.

"Monogram Pictures Presents: 'Rotten Together'—starring Fay Wray and King Kong's mother."

"You think it's funny? You bastard—" and for the first time in thirty-six years, Sally slapped her little boy hard across the face.

"The two of you—you're a couple of kids who need somebody should wash out your mouths for you. When are you going to realize you've got a kid of your own to think about," and she walked out into the hall, Honey calling after her:

"Well, it's a good thing she's got you, then, isn't it?" Bitter, angry, jealous, desperate, frustrated, hopeless, helpless.

"Hey—comeon," Lenny said, looking up from his stupor.

"Be a pal—kiss and make up you two," and he was out again—and then in.

"You gotta get up, Lenny, Chicago's waitin' for you. Nah, I don't wanna get up," and he slumps down on the floor again. In his raincoat. In his shoes with no socks, with that eight o'clock shadow on him that draws the black of his eyes down the front of his face.

"I don't wanna get up."

Except that what he wanna or don't wanna don't cut no ice with the owner of the club.

"Forcrissakes," she screams at Sally, who's trying to get a stay of execution for Lenny. "What do you want from my life? I got five bucks a head out there —look at them."

And she looks. The place is crowded. O.K., they're not so chic anymore. But there's a lot of them and they paid their money to see Lenny Bruce in top form or in trouble—either way.

"I don't care if the guy pees in his pants up there. He's goin' on."

While peeing in his pants turns out to be only the start—after which the guy can't seem to manage the right button with the right buttonhole. While Honey stares into the mirror over the dressing table and lays out *The Girl of the Limberlost* five-year-plan for them.

"You know what we're gonna do, Lenny? We're gonna take our daughter. We're gonna take Kitty up to the woods, just you and her—and me and nature, know what I mean? Lenny, nature's the only way for people to have a real relationship. You know what I mean?" Tracing her reflection in the glass. Going over all the "down" lines with her broken fingernail.

"Lenny?"

Black-eyed, roughed-over Lenny, who must have puked in his raincoat before he peed—he's peering out from behind a drape into the arena, a Christian counting the lions.

"See 'em? The State heat, the County heat, the city heat—and that's gotta be two guys from Interpol."

"Lenny, I'm not hooked on anything. Honest. I can quit anytime I want to," watching him drag his filthy bones her way, fumbling with the buttons, unable to get them anywhere near the holes. And there's a moment when she focuses on him, when she recognizes the total truth in their lives. But it passes.

The band finishes.

He shakes the shit out of his eyes.

"Ahhhh—King Kong is ready," and he forces out a gorilla bit that comes crossed with a weasel. Over the drumroll the PA system introduces, "Ladies and Gentlemen: Lenny Bruce," and out he goes: a dreg. One very used, very beat-up, dirty old dreg, into the breech for posterity.

He shuffles into the spotlight, grabs the mike and gives his benediction.

"Superjew" he calls into the glaring light. He bends his head, waiting. For what? He catches himself and is suddenly sure he must say something else. Go fuck yourselves? No. No, that's not it. It's, Oh yeah—

Yeah—King Kong's ready now. Well he's almost ready if the band knows what I mean. We're having King for the second show and I just want to warn the photographers to cool the flashbulbs—otherwise he gets a little shitty, uh—yeah, just give him a building to play with—and a plane and—uh

The heat. Boy it's really getting to him. The lights in his eyes. Why doesn't somebody get the fucking light out of his eyes. How's he supposed to think.

Oh yeah—you know the Ecumenical council has given the Pope permission to become a nun. Only on Fridays though. Yeah—Where, yeah—

I told you about the lights. Shut the fucking lights off.

Yeah, see a judge—Now a judge can get away with losing his place. Like man, he can be so dunced up out there, but—you know, he don't know where he is, he's been doing the racing form under the brief there. He's—Sure—He just harrumps a couple of times and—Yeah—Well, I'll take that under advisement. Sure—Lessee what was I doing?

And he's reeling around up there, from one side of the stage to the other, pickle-tongued and, oh boy, is life Mickey Mantle over and over again. You hit 'em out of the ballpark and they write your name all over cereal boxes, but screw up once Charlie and your blood ain't all they want. Your cracked skull, spit in your eyeball, a knee in your groin—

"Yer in there to hit 'em over the fence boy. Hit 'em over the fence," and don't think you can lay your problems on me, fella. That ain't my problem.

Be funny Lenny.

The reason I'm wearing my raincoat. As most of

you know, I've been getting busted a lot lately for obscenity, and the last two times—Frisco and then L.A.—they didn't give me a chance to get my coat. And since Chicago is a cold town—Yeah, the windy city—So I'm ready, you know. Hey, any attorneys here tonight? Any attorneys?

And one guy raises his hand.

"Beautiful," he says, reaches into his pocket, pulls out a couple of bucks, plus a couple of other things, and tosses the money to the attorney.

Now you've got it all.

Three people snicker and then he points to the cops, writing as fast as their little blue fingers can carry them.

Willya look at them. They're stealing my act as fast as they can. Gonna break it out in Vegas—in the lounge.

He looks down at the stuff he's pulled from his pocket. A couple of cocktail napkins with phone numbers on them, a crumpled Coke cup, a wallet. He starts to put them away and then thinks twice about the wallet.

Wanna see a beautiful pink-nippled lady, my wife— Yeah, let's see, where is she?

And he rummages through the photos.

Oh yeah (and his voice trails off) —I gave her away, I remember—

The couple at the first table have had it by this time. They get up.

Hey, where you goin' you guys? I haven't even said "cocksucker" yet. Never mind, let them go. Let the Bear hump them.

And somebody else somewhere else gets ugly.

Hey comeon—I can't work this shithouse. My head is killing me, see—I'll tell you where it's at. O.K., take Catholicism it's a franchise see—Ever heard of *Howard Johnson's?* And Kennedy—yeah, baby, that's where it's at. And—where else? Well, I was supposed to open at a club down the street, and ah, someone—we're not naming names here—someone took out all the toilets. And do you know it is illegal to have a club without a toilet. I know what you're thinking: "Ah, he's a nut." I'll Nut you! What do you know about it. I tell you I'm talking about harass—harassment, repression—I'm talking about club owners who get phone calls in the middle of the night and are afraid to hire me. I'm talking about Vietnam, baby—atrocities—

And suddenly he stops. His face turns from fury to smiles.

Oh yeah, I know what I wanted to show you.

He reaches into his pocket again and pulls out a ripped clip from a Chicago newspaper.

—article here in the paper about these transvestites who are posing as policemen. Here's Officer Dolan (Lenny does his fag act, very broad, very lispy): Stan—as the guys down at the baths call him—"Officer Stanley Dolan said the hardest part was learning to walk in high heels." See—

He waves at the police.

You're naive, you guys. I usually go out of my way to defend you guys but you *are* naive. You figure the guy'll grab one of you and you'll say, "O.K. now, I'm not a beautiful girl—I'm a Police Officer with Chicago's Finest." But dig it, you don't know who you're dealing with—

RAPIST: I don't care if you're a cop. You got a cute ass, baby.

See? They'll just *shtup* you baby. No—see now that's not very nice—ah, to—a—yeah, entrap—no, to incite—No—Look folks, I'm sorry I'm just not funny tonight. Sometimes I'm not funny, I'm just Lenny Bruce.

And he's sick. It's almost literary, his getting sick, just then. Pathetic fallacy, straight out of Thomas Hardy. The storm when things are all churned up at home. The high wind when the child has lost its way. And now, as Lenny leaves the stage with no applause and no act and no nothing—he's sick.

"See ma?" he says backstage. "And you were so worried? Listen to that ovation." He slams into the toilet and pukes up his guts. The two plainclothesmen ready to lay another bust on him hardly give him the time to get to the dry heaves.

"Hey, what's wrong with you people anyway. This is America, Jim. You can't come into my shithouse without a warrant—"

Except they're in and Lenny passes out all over their feet.

CHAPTER 37

BAD TIMES AND THEN MORE OF THE SAME.

"But specifically," the interviewer asked Honey.

"Well, specifically, I don't really know any longer. You know—I was sick. The different places all seemed the same, you know. Kinda all blended together. I can't remember anymore which ones were jails and which were hospitals."

Then he asked Sally.

"Well let's see. Lenny. He was in and out of hospitals. He had this abscess. Bad. I mean it wasn't all with the drugs and everything, the kid was really sick. One time, one time in particular I didn't think he was gonna make it."

And from Artie, the interviewer heard what he'd figured anyway.

"Everybody'd heard about Lenny by then; nobody wanted to book him. But I kept at it, and finally got him a gig—and he went over. They really dug him. And he got off on that. But later, after the gig, somebody slipped him some LSD without telling him and

he ended up goin' out a window. You know, the guy
thought he could fly."

That's one version.

"Who're you shittin'?" The cop who scooped him
up off the sidewalk.

"Looks like horse to me."

"What horse? You dumb bastard, the guy's dyin'
here—"

"Hijo de la puta!" Lenny's screaming, grabbing at
any moving parts, waving his arms around—huddled
over his own mass of broken bones. His ankles, his
thighs, his shoulders. Crunched, twisted—out the window on something.

"Get down, Lenny. Lenny forcrissakes get off the
window sill!" Out of his persecuted head; everywhere
he looked, cops, laws, wagging index fingers down his
craw. Arrested for speeding, arrested for possession,
arrested for opening his yap, leave him alone already,
one trial after another, sailing though the clean air,
the sonavabitch so goddammed lucky he didn't land
on his head.

"Yeah? So who needs it anyway?" he raved. Raved,
wept, hurt, broke and splattered.

His friend begging the man: "What's the difference
what he's on, the guy's fractured—can't you see the
parts coming apart everywhere?"

"I seen the two a youse guys. I seen him kissin' you,
and you kissin' him back."

"Pick him up, you mother—pick the bastard up off
the pavement, get him an ambulance—I love you Lenny. Lenny you dumb motherfucker, I love you."
Some friend, any friend—a friend in the path, from
one scene or another. He tried to stop him. He grabbed
for his ankles before he fell.

Fell or jumped.

Jumped or flew—

Before he landed like a trick diver, somersaulting

in the air to land on his feet three stories down, where he drove his legs halfway up his body to his head like a couple of nails in a coffin—screaming, cursing, crying and out-of-it all the way.

CHAPTER 38

ABBOTT AND COSTELLO
Elizabeth and Mary
Kafka and Bruce—
Who could believe anybody would pick up, mend
and be back in it again. Back with the headlines. With
the trouble. With the spritz.

He'd cadged another club owner willing to risk a
bust, so was back in business but under threat of im-
minent FORECLOSURE; the word was out.

1964 *Cafe Au Go Go*. New York City.

But comeon, everybody loves a suicide. Once again
Lenny found himself with a very hip audience—when
they could find a seat. Most of those were taken up
with the butts of the law.

What was it with those nuts in blue? They get
evicted from their corner saloons? They got nowhere else to hang out?

O.K.!

He waves the transcripts from his recent trials in front of the audience.

Ready or not, here comes Lucky Lenny—hey never-mind. You know there's been an obscenity circus that's been going on now about four years. And you know it's killing me. It's killing me and I really can't believe it's not settled.

(He rattles the papers in front of a couple's face.) Hey look—from '61 on, came the arguments between the petulant lower court judges, the Supreme Court and spoiled rotten DA's. The city attorney in L.A.? Every time he'd lose in Washington, I'd get my ass kicked in when he got home. Like—O.K., I have this horrible persistent fantasy that one day I'll walk out onto a stage and the entire audience will be nothing but cops. Yeah—O.K., where was I? Oh yeah, Chicago bust. Guilty, right? And that case is being appealed to the Illinois Supreme Court, on the grounds that—

And he's losing a lot of them—don't tell them grounds. You think they got into the *Au Go Go* on accounta their sweet smiles? They paid up, Lenny. Now you pay up—let's have a few laughs.

What? Yeah, you. Wake up, you—these are the jokes. What? You want a bit? You want my Lenny Bruce impression, is that it?

"Comeon Lenny. Do 'Tits and Ass,' 'How to Make Your Colored Friends Relaxed at a Party.' "

Screw tits and ass. You wanna know where it's at with tits, I'll tell ya. See that chick over there? Now she has beautiful tits. You really do, dear. Bless you. Bless you.

He does his mike benediction routine. Then he digresses a minute on his famous: I'd rather my kids watch a stag movie where the only violence is administered with a pillow—under her ass—rather than the

King of Kings flick, with all the crucifixions, and
the bleeding palms, the thorns forced into the forehead—the sadism number. Then he makes with a little Johnson and Lady Bird and he's back to the dame
with the nice knockers.

But no way could we take a picture of those tits and
put it on a newspaper—that's where tits are at. The
only pictures of tits you see in the paper is tits that
have been strafed, shot up, napalmed—maimed.
Yeah. That's really weird. Stage movies are bad.
Napalm is good. Weird.

A couple of the faithful in the corner are stamping
their feet. O.K. so he's not funny. What's there to be
funny about? But the rest are generally up and down
like the Duncan yo-yo. He almost had them with the
stag movie stuff. The big green for loveable Lyndon
but the minute he comes on with the lecture routine
again, it's eighty-six with the big weights. They came
for Lenny to tickle their attention spans; to read the
editorial page of the *New York Post* they don't have
to up a minimum.

And then it happens. The big blue ballet. Everybody's really happy. Now that's what they really call
entertainment. As the first cops start for the stage. As
Lenny comes through, the in-person martyr-myth in
person. And now everybody's a hundred percenter. To
a customer.

"Can we have the lights on in here?"

"Again?"

Just the sound of the surprise, chagrin, fear, terror
and fury in Lenny's "again?" A quick shot of *Geritol*,
as the plot starts to really thicken.

"What the fuck's going on? It's chic to arrest me?
I mean what did I do wrong this time?"

"Ladies and gentlemen, would you take out any
ID you have with you"—and it's instant Clyde Beatty.
The cops are moving like The FBI At Peace And
Holocaust. The faithful are starting in with the nap-

kin missiles. There's catcalls. There's frenzy. There's real genuine audience participation with a vengeance—the cover charge has come through.

"She *does* have beautiful tits."

"O.K., Lenny, the show's over."

"Well what's wrong with saying it?"

"—come on—" grabbing the mike so that Lenny has to shout, "You got beautiful tits, lady. What's wrong with saying it?"

"Lenny, let's go."

"Under what statute are you arresting me?"

"Aw come on, Lenny."

"No. I wanna know. What statute?"

"O.K., 1140. Now let's go."

"Screw 1140. 1140's prostitution."

"Well, whatever it is—"

"Well, let's at least be accurate, man. It's 1140A—'A'—ya dig? Giving an indecent performance. O.K.?"

"O.K." And it's back into yet another courtroom and life has gotten to be trial out, year in. You get up in the morning. Read some Cardozo. Run down a gig. Beat your chops. Take off a minute and geeze. Another to beat your meat and it's back to the books again. Section Something, Article Something Else. He turns around and another cop is on the stand. Another cop looks down at his notes. Another cop tells another judge and another jury just what it was in particular that caused him to drag in Dirty Lenny for the seventh time in three years.

"It's over, Lenny," they're singing in the wind. "All that's left is to roll over and live up to the part."

It's not news anymore. Who wants to hang around in a courtroom watching Lenny get shafted? "Like it's tough shit, fella, but dig it—it sucks, man." So the courtroom got lonely. Sure, a lot of fancy civil-libertarians signed petitions in his day, and a lot of fancy civil-libertarians hung around hanging on his every move testifying and adoring him. For a while. But after a while even some of them thought he ought to cool it. Maybe they wouldn't go so far as to say it sucks. But there were so *many* pressing injustices crowding their social calendars. So many causes to embrace.

So there he is again. In between two *new* attorneys. One uptown good-schools obscenity expert, white; and his up-and-mobile black assistant, who mostly has to remind Lenny to cool it, and then cool it some more. Because Lenny has long since forgotten how to shut up and let the halfback carry his ball for him.

"What are you paying me for, you dumb SOB," as the cop testifies that,

"The subject stated that Eleanor Roosevelt gave the clap to Lou Gehrig" and Lenny interrupted with, "Ah, c'mon, man—That's so out of context."

His lawyer then interrupted Lenny with some high-priced legal advice. "Shut up, Lenny," said his lawyer. "Shut up, Lenny, Shut up, Lenny."

And back to the witness stand.

"Some of this is not in sequence, your Honor."

"Just what you recall, Officer."

"Well then he said," the cop said that Lenny said, "that it was nice to say, 'Fuck You,' to people," which got Lenny to his feet again.

"Comeon, buddy—if you're gonna say it, then do the whole bit."

At which point the judge got that red look around his eyes.

"Counsel will control their client."

He said "client" as if it had a capital K in front of it. And then a nod to the cop, who continued with, "I'm sorry, your Honor. The subject talked so fast, when he was performing—"

"That's quite all right, Officer. Just give the court your revived recollections."

"Yes, sir." (Checking his notes.) "Oh yes, and then he said that President Johnson stood around in his underwear at night waiting for his wife—no,—*begging* his wife to 'touch it.' And—let's see. Oh yeah—stag movies."

"What did he say about stag movies?"

"Well, he said they were good—"

While Lenny turned on a spit, staring at the ceiling, slapping his forehead, thinking to himself, what's the good to get up in the morning?

"Well actually what he said was that the stag movies were better for kids to watch than *King of Kings,* and—"

"What else?" said the DA. (Kindly voice, an "I-don't-know—you-tell-me," look at the jury.)

"What else?"

"Well, at one point he complimented a young lady on her breasts."

"Breasts? Is that the word he used?"

"Well—" (Blushing.) "Well—" (Lowering his voice and avoiding the eyes of the jury.) "Well, actually he said, tits—and then made a gesture at her."

"What sort of gesture?"

"Well, it was a gesture with the microphone."

"Would you please demonstrate for the court?"

"It was—ah—like this," he said and started to act out a vigorous wacking off, which really wigged Lenny out.

"Gettatahere!" he screamed. "I never—I never meant that to mean jackoff and you know it—"

As the judge goes into a rapping fit and the attorneys try the "now, now" routine with him, all of which leave him fit to be tied in a knot as he moves towards the bench.

"It's pathetic. I mean face it—he's doing my act for you and he's bombing. Forgodsakes, man—you've been on twenty minutes. You haven't got one *fablunged* laugh, right?"

"Mr. Bruce!"

"I mean, couldn't one of you guys give him a little direction? Cue him, teach him something about projection. The guy's terrible. Hey, your Honor—Now how can you make a fair judgment based on this? Yeah, what he's doing *is* obscene—but that's not my routine. They do have what you call 'redeeming social value.' And if anyone is going to do my act, it should be *me*. I ought to be able to do me a lot better than he does me. After all, I've been at it longer—"

(As the DA blows air on his fingertips. As the judge bangs his gavel and clenches his mind.)

"This court is recessed. We'll reconvene at eleven o'clock. I want defense counsel in my chambers right now."

(As Lenny's lawyers wonder if the loss of one case will permanently damage their careers.)

Lenny hounding them. Lenny following them out to the john, Lenny haranguing them over the walls of the cubbies.

"If I could just talk to him, you know—eye to eye. I just know he's not a bad guy. I could make him come around, I'm telling you. He's got it in him. I know he's got it in him."

"Forcrissakes Bruce, the guy's a tough sonavabitch who doesn't want word one from you. The next time you open your yap he'll cite you for contempt and get out of the way—I wanna, forcrissakes, wash my hands, forcrissakes—"

"But then you guys are not representing me the way I want to be represented. Did you talk to him about *me* doing the act for him, instead of the cop?"

"Didn't you hear the man, Jim?" (Attorney #2.) "We've been over that a hundred times."

"And we feel—" (Back to Attorney #1). "We told you what we feel. We feel that would be comple—"

"Yeah, I know—completely detrimental to my case, except you're wrong. I'm telling ya that unless I do the act for him myself I'm gonna lose."

"O.K.," they say.

What the hell, the guy's in traction anyway. Especially after the chapter and verse they got from the judge in his chambers, including respect for the law, this is not a rumpus room, dignity, flags and two more choruses, in stereo and living color.

"OK. We'll have to eat the Guilty verdict here and we'll appeal, that's all. We'll appeal."

"What do you mean eat? Oh, you guys are wild. For you it's an afternoon at Nedicks while I do the time, right?"

"Hey, Lenny, calm your ass. It'll be like Chicago. You'll get satisfaction from the State Supreme Court."

"Sure. Look you mugs, Chicago took almost two years and every nickel I had in the bank. You guys don't understand. I'm like a nigger in Alabama—lookin' to use the toilet and by the time I get some satisfaction it's gonna be too late. I don't wanna go to jail, and—I'll tell you something else—either put me on the stand and let me do my act for the court, or I'm gonna put a lien on the files, sue your asses, and go in there and represent myself—ya dig?"

"Yeah, we dig—and frankly, Lenny, it's A.O.K., because you, man, are nothing but a *big* pain in the ass. And anytime you want the files, just up the $14,000 you owe and you know what you can do with them."

"And—as for feeling like a nigger in Alabama, baby—you don't have a clue as to what that feels like."

"Oh yeah?" Lenny says, looking at the good-looking black face looking at him, and its Brooks Brothers suit, and its button-down aspirations. "Well neither do you, Jim—so forget it."

CHAPTER 39

ONE DAY HAS FOLLOWED ANOTHER. LENNY HAS SOME-
how gotten himself up in the morning and stood for
too long in front of the mirror. The bloated dissolute
who faced him had a distant familiarity about him.
Familiar but not quite recognizable. (The sheik swal-
lowed by Daniel's whale.) The whale sneered at him.
He put on something and got out of there. The smell
of closeness was too much for him.

"Mr. Bruce," said the judge. He was rapping his
gavel. "It has come to my attention that you have
dismissed your counsel."

"Yes, your Honor." Your Honor, your Honor, he
stared at him. Your Honor, you are taking over my
life, you are disguising my body, you are digesting my
intentions. These walls, the twelve men and women
of my peers who follow me into my toilet, who sit
on the base of my spine as I reach towards sleep
through a haze of prescriptions, you are—

"Yes, your Honor. I am substituting for counsel."
I will be heard. I will be justified, your Honor—I—

"Mr. Bruce, you should not appear in this court without suitable counsel."

Suitable, suitable, two pairs of pants, feel the goods —suitable for the crowned heads of—

"I urge you to retain new counsel. I will even—"

"If it please the court. I wish to defend myself. I wish—"

"If you are making a request that I grant you a continuance Mr. Bruce, in order for you to retain new counsel, then I will so grant that request."

If you wish to retain new counsel Mr. Bruce. If you wish to retain new—

"Please, your Honor—I just want a chance to talk to the court. You know, just to talk. To another human being, without all the legal doubletalk and—bullshit—"

And again with the gavel rapping. It goes through his guts, bang bang bang, the sounds of all the lawbooks, the unintelligible syntax of a misinformed computer—

"Mr. Bruce."

My name is Lenny.

"Would you please sit down."

Everybody calls me Lenny. Everybody—"Look all these attorneys keep telling me 'Ah, don't worry, it's just a lower court.' They're all assholes—we lose here, we'll win in the higher court. What is this bullshit?"

As the gavel raps louder and louder through his head.

"But I don't believe I *should* lose here because I don't believe I'm doing anything wrong."

"Mr. Bruce!"

"I mean, I believe I have the right to say the things I'm saying."

"Mr. Bruce—I am running out of patience."

Listen to me, willya? Ya got your fingers up your ears? Listen to me; dontcha get off work anytime in that head of yours?

"Your Honor—if you'd just let me do my act for

the court—I'll take my chances. If after you hear me do it, if you don't think it's funny—if it just strikes you as 'dirty' or 'obscene'—"

"I cannot allow this to continue."

Give me a break, you bastard. Look at me.

"Look—I know you're a good person—and I—I mean it—I genuinely want your respect. Look, I know this legal system is the best in the world—but you can't *hear* me."

Nobody in this goddamn room's listening to me, look at them, with those Sunday Go-to-High-and-Mighty expressions on them.

"Dontcha see, when I talk about 'Tits and Ass' I'm not up there just to shock the audience by repeating the words tits and ass, tits and ass—the point I'm trying to make your Honor, is that we live in a hypocritical society where—"

"Mr. Bruce! You leave me no alternative but to find you in contempt of court."

Contempt of court, making in your pants, sneezing in your milk, spitting in the subway—go ahead, find me—I'm guilty. We're guilty, my family, we killed him. Signed Morty, he didn't wanna become a doctor.

"Then sentence me—I have no money left. Might I be sentenced now? Go ahead, I can't afford to stay in this city. I can't work here. The police took away my cabaret card. Please—Sentence me."

"No, I will not sentence you today. This case has not been properly tried. I order you when you appear in front of me again to appear with suitable counsel and I am further ordering a psychiatric evaluation by the psychiatric clinic. December 16th. Bail continued."

"Your Honor—" Honorable Honor, your honor sir. "You're trying to stop the information!"

"May I have an officer of the court up here?"

As Lenny, the lemming who's already been dealt the final clobber, pushes ever forward towards the bench. Who's going on and on over the banging, over

171

the Court Officer's admonitions—Over all sense of, it's finished Lenny, lie down and let them cart you away.

"See—That's where it's at, stopping the information. Well you can't—The information keeps the country strong. You need the deviate. Don't shut him up. The madman—You need him to stand up and tell you if you're blowing it. And the harder—"

Arms, legs, around him, hand over his mouth.

"The harder you come down on him, the more you need him." Need him—You, out there—me, deviate— Need. Getcha fuckin hands off, you bastard—all I want to do is get a chance to say something forcrissakes. What's so terrible about that?"

CHAPTER 40

THE LAST TIME THE INTERVIEWER TALKED TO HONEY was in the library of Lenny's ex-house. It was refurnished. Owned by someone else. They talked about the time when it was crowded with the lawbooks that didn't seem to ever amount to the right answers for the guy. When it was still strewn with the tapes, transcripts and electronic equipment that came to add up to Lenny. When the sound of her voice echoed through the large empty building that kind of hung around waiting for a reason to be there.

"—the analyst explained that I felt—insecure—and inadequate and all. He said it probably had to do with the fact that—well that Lenny had grown so famous and all and I felt terribly left behind, you know. That, like I hadn't grown at all. I was functioning, he said, like a child and that's why I was doing all those terrible things. They were called—let's see—Oh yeah— 'Attention-getting devices.'"

When he spoke to Sally he asked her about the house.

"I understand they found a letter from the bank telling him he'd lost the place. Is that true?"

"Yeah."

"This house meant a lot to Lenny, didn't it?"

"Yeah."

"Can you tell me how he reacted when the letter came?"

"Hey, comeon with this—I know what you're leading to and forget it. I mean cut it out with that crap, Lenny loved life. He was convinced he'd be completely exonerated. And he was. That's all. Wasn't he?"

Artie said he loved the guy. He also said he was very happy his records were selling so well again.

But all that was way later.

Way after the cops and the photographers and the famous picture of Lenny on the bathroom floor.

CHAPTER 41

IN OCTOBER OF 1965 LENNY WAS DECLARED A LEGAL pauper.

In November he listened to Kitty sing. He said, "I loved it, man. You were too much."

So was he. He was fat enough for three Lenny Bruces.

"Bye, man," his kid said to him as she went off with Gramma Sally, blowing kisses out the back window of the car, in August, 1966.

Everything's not as good as it once was. The linoleum's coming up in the kitchen. The car needs a valve job. The bank told him "Too bad, buddy," on the house number. They were coming to take it back again, Lenny's Marion Davies dream on the hill, where he walked from room to room with a tape recorder in his pocket taking down the sounds of the dripping faucet, the sounds of the needles going into his arms, legs, eyebrows, knees, ankles, teeth—the sounds of what was left of him. The sounds of all the hangeroners who were still hanging around.

The sounds of Honey, stripping again.

The sounds of his death.

Lying on the floor of the crapper, with the rag still around his wrist, the works still lying around the floor.

Lenny OD'd on his own time and place, this time beating the system for real. You just ain't supposed to step out of that great chain of being. You're supposed to hang around, knowing your place and staying in line. That's the way to live past forty. To please the gavel-rappers up there who pull your strings for you.

Except for once Lenny had it his way.